I can feel that this is wrong.

Don't any of you feel it?
Something awful is about
to happen.

AGAINST THE TIDE

AGAINST THE TIDE

Tui T. Sutherland

SCHOLASTIC INC.

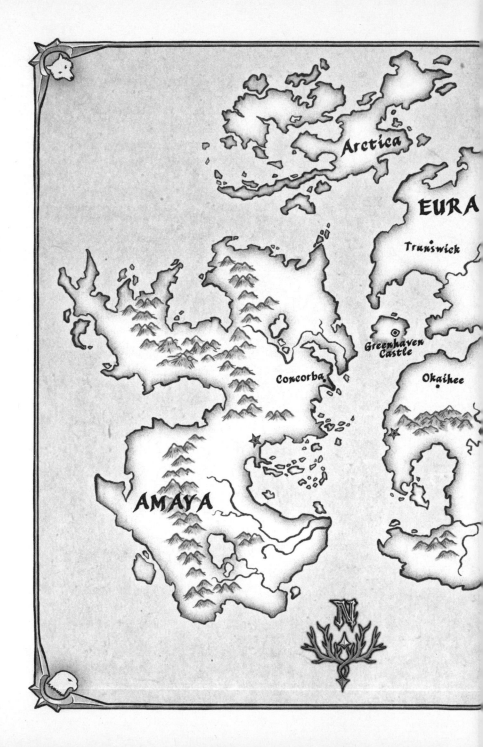

Library of Congress Control Number: 2014940799

ISBN 978-0-545-52247-2
10 9 8 7 6 5 4 3 2 1   14 15 16 17 18

Book design by Charice Silverman
Map illustration by Michael Walton

First edition, October 2014

Printed in the U.S.A.   110

Scholastic US: 557 Broadway • New York, NY 10012
Scholastic Canada: 604 King Street West • Toronto, ON M5V 1E1
Scholastic New Zealand Limited: Private Bag 94407 • Greenmount, Manukau 2141
Scholastic UK Ltd.: Euston House • 24 Eversholt Street • London NW1 1DB

For Elliot and Jonah, and for my
spirit animal, Sunshine
— T.S.

1

KOVO

THE PEOPLE OF STETRIOL CALLED IT MUTTERING ROCK.
They knew vaguely where it was, deep in the scorched, arid interior of the continent. They knew of the muttering sound that made the earth tremble for miles in all directions around it.

And they knew the name of the dark, sinister creature imprisoned there.

Most of all, they knew never to go anywhere near it if they wanted to survive.

So no one had visited Kovo the Ape's prison in hundreds of years. Not that it would be easy, if anyone had even wanted to try. Muttering Rock was far out in the Stetriol desert, many days from the nearest source of water. Each side of the rock was a sheer cliff face with no handholds, as if someone had sliced away the edges with one swipe of a powerful blade.

The top of the rock was baked by the sun to a blistering two hundred degrees or so – no one had ever measured the exact temperature, of course, but it was enough to instantly and badly burn any foot, or boot, or paw that tried to step onto it.

The cage itself seemed to be growing out of the top of the rock, a vast network of impenetrable branches as hard as diamonds. It glowed a pure, blinding white, particularly at its sharpest points, where it still had the vague shape of the giant antlers planted centuries ago by the Great Beast Tellun.

And of course, there was the eagle overhead: Halawir, the sharp-eyed guard who watched Kovo every day and all night too.

So: no visitors. Not in a very, very long time.

Hence the muttering.

"First I will peel off their skin," growled a voice like thunder in the distant mountains. "I will crush their skulls between my fists. I will wrap their bones in their green cloaks and set fire to their homes. Their fortresses will be dust beneath my feet."

The malevolent eyes of an enormous silverback gorilla glowered through the gaps in the cage. His thick black fur was heavy in the heat. There was no room in his cage for pacing, so he sat, brooding and waiting, as he had for generations. Kings and empires had risen and fallen since his imprisonment, but still, he waited.

And while he waited, he dreamed of vengeance.

"I have killed four Great Beasts," he murmured. "When I am free, I will punish those presumptuous Greencloaks who follow them. I will tear their spirit animals apart and then I will kill all the feeble humans myself. Some of them I will strangle slowly, and others I will drown, and some I will crush beneath my feet." He brushed one leathery palm against the antlers that hemmed him in.

In the distance, a bird of prey shrieked, piercing and desperate in the broiling air.

"Not much longer. Worthless humans. If I were free, we'd have all the talismans already. We'd be the kings of this world and everyone would bow to us."

His colossal muscles rippled as he pushed against the cage walls. "Soon. My time is coming. They'll come for me soon," he muttered, squinting out at the small square of empty desert he could see. "Gerathon has been free for weeks. Slow, despicable humans. Perhaps I will rip off their toes."

He lifted his head, his giant nostrils flaring as he sniffed the air. A slow, cunning smile spread across his face.

"Gerathon," he rumbled. "At last."

"I understand your eagerness to spill the blood of your enemies," said a voice from behind him. "But after the centuries you've already waited, what does another month or two matter?"

"I will wait as long as I have to for my plans to come to bear," said Kovo. "Stand where I can see you."

A brown-haired boy inched into view and stopped a few steps away from the cage, not far from the sheer edge of the cliff behind him. He was thin and small, barely old enough to drink the Bile, and terribly sunburned. Long, bleeding scratches marked his shoulders, and he didn't seem to notice the smoke rising from the burning soles of his shoes. But perhaps that had something to do with who was really inside him, looking out through snakelike yellow eyes, pupils huge and dilated.

"An unusually small creature for you," Kovo growled. "Looks more like one of your snacks than a messenger." He glanced at the sky, but there was no sign of Halawir. Useful timing, that: his ever-watchful guard missing right on time for his visitor.

"Oh, I am sure I shall eat him later," the boy said, and although it was not Gerathon's voice, not exactly, there was still an eerie hiss to it that echoed the serpentine Great Beast. "Sssso . . . it's been a long time. What have you been up to?"

"Terribly amusing," Kovo snarled. His dark eyes gleamed from deep beneath his forbidding brow. "Did you come here to flaunt your freedom?"

"No," Gerathon said, almost sympathetically, for her. "I came to tell you how well we're doing. The Conquerors just stole the Crystal Polar Bear from those scruffy Greencloak midgets. Plus I was able to do some entertaining mental torture on one of them, since his mother is one of my creatures. Oh, his *face* when she tried to kill him. It was *delightful*."

"Marvelous," said Kovo. "Leave me here for eons if you like, just as long as you're having fun."

"Your time for fun is coming too," Gerathon said, covering the boy's mouth as she made him yawn deliberately. "We have almost enough talismans to free you."

"That is . . . *almost* what I want to hear," Kovo said with glittering menace.

"Trust me," Gerathon said languidly. "We have our ways of knowing everything the Greencloaks do, and we know exactly where the Four Fallen are going next. As always. We'll get the next talisman, and then we'll destroy them."

"I notice you haven't destroyed them yet," Kovo pointed out. "Care to explain why they're still alive?"

Gerathon waved the boy's hand dismissively. "They're still useful to me. To *us*. To our Reptile King. Don't worry, they'll all be dead soon."

The boy suddenly let out a cry of pain and fell forward onto his hands and knees. Scorching burns immediately blistered along his skin.

"Oh, curses," Gerathon hissed, a weirdly calm voice coming out of a face contorted with agony. "This pathetic little costume isn't going to be much use to me for much longer. Perhaps I should call back his buzzard to carry him away."

"Ah," Kovo said. "That's how you got him up here."

"Yes. We chose the smallest human and bonded him with the Bile to a giant bird," she answered. Kovo squinted at the sky and saw large wings circling—not Halawir's, for once.

The boy collapsed completely, and the sizzling smell of burning hair filled the air. "Ah, well," Gerathon went on, "this one's almost dead. How boring of him. I suppose this is good-bye for now, Kovo."

"Wait," he growled, clutching at the antlers. "How much longer will I be stuck in here?"

"Next time I see you," she hissed, her voice fading as the boy's eyes closed and the life drained from his body, "we will *both* be free.

"And then . . . all of Erdas will be ours."

2

AT SEA

*I*T'S SO CLOSE.

Abeke stared across the dark, rushing waves at the shore slipping past them. The afternoon sun was warm against her skin and cast bright golden sparkles along the ocean, but the wind was colder than it seemed like it should be.

Nilo. My home. My family.

All she could see of it was a strip of beach and thick green jungle beyond. This part of Nilo didn't look anything like the dry savannah around her village, but it was still as close to home as she had been in a long time.

I wonder what Soama would think if she could see me now. Or Father. Abeke rubbed the wound in her left shoulder where a Conqueror had buried a knife during their last battle. It had healed enough for her to use her bow again — a new bow, to replace the one shattered by a Conqueror's war hammer — but it still ached sometimes, especially when the air was chilly. *Would my family be proud of me after all this? Or would they still think I'm a disgrace and a disappointment?*

She tugged her green cloak closer around her shoulders and reached out, almost unconsciously, for her leopard.

"Rrrreowr," Uraza grumbled, shoving her head under Abeke's hand. The leopard sat for a moment, letting Abeke stroke her fur and glaring balefully at the ocean. Then she sprang up again and went back to pacing up and down the ship with long, rolling strides.

Maybe I'm only feeling out of sorts because she is, Abeke thought. Uraza, like most cats — giant or otherwise — strongly disliked water, particularly enormous bodies of water, and most particularly enormous bodies of water that surrounded her on all sides and smelled of fish she couldn't catch herself.

"I know," Abeke whispered, watching her spirit animal pace. "I wish we were back on land too." It was hard to be cooped up on the ship for so long, but Tarik insisted that going all the way around Nilo was the safest route to Oceanus. The usual sea route — the passage between Nilo and Zhong — was sure to be swarming with Conquerors now.

Abeke was about to call Uraza back and offer her the choice of going into passive state, but right at that moment, Jhi the giant panda emerged from belowdecks directly into the leopard's path.

Startled, Uraza leaped back and snarled, raising her hackles. Her teeth gleamed ferociously in the sunlight and her claws left gouges in the wooden boards of the deck.

"Uraza!" Abeke called.

Jhi blinked placidly at the leopard and then turned to amble away. But behind her was Meilin, who scowled at Uraza with one hand on the knife at her waist.

"She didn't mean any harm," Abeke said, hurrying up to them. She put a calming hand on Uraza's back. "She's just jumpy. We all are."

"I wonder why," Meilin said. Abeke knew what she meant, of course: another lost talisman, another pointless journey, and the little matter of Rollan's news that someone was passing information to the enemy. Meilin looked hard at Abeke for a moment, then added, "Do us all a favor and learn to control your bad-tempered cat."

Uraza hissed softly as Meilin stalked away.

"It's all right," Abeke whispered, stroking the leopard's fur. "I understand why she's worried." *But I'm not the mole. I'm loyal to the Greencloaks. Yes, I like Shane and happen to think he's not totally evil, but—I would never, never betray my friends.*

It wouldn't be betraying them if I went home, though, would it?

For a moment she let herself follow that fantasy. She could sneak up onto the deck in the middle of the night, borrow one of the small rowboats, lower it over the side . . . and strike off for Nilo on her own, gone before anyone even noticed. She knew she could survive the trek back to her village, using her hunting skills and the bond with Uraza that made her swifter and stronger than ever.

Meilin would be relieved to find me gone. Rollan too, probably. And why should I stay with people who don't trust me? She squinted up at the sun, thinking of Conor. She thought Conor would miss her . . . and she knew she would miss him. Back in Arctica, he'd said *being with you is like being with family.* Except that Abeke's family usually made her feel uncomfortable and small and worthless, while being with Conor was easy and warm.

But she was still worried about them—her father and Soama. Her whole village, in fact. What if they needed her and Uraza to protect them?

Uraza growled under her fingertips, and Abeke wondered if the leopard had guessed her thoughts. "Oh, I won't do it," she said, crouching to talk to her spirit animal. "No need to make that bossy face at me. I'm not an idiot; I saw what happened when Conor and Meilin chose their families over our quest—and when Rollan nearly did. I *know* the best way to protect Father and Soama is to find the talismans and stop the Devourer."

She sighed. *Besides, my family would probably be about as pleased to see me as Meilin usually is. "Oh, you're back, are you? The Greencloaks didn't want you either? Well, of course you failed. We knew that was going to happen. And don't even think about bringing that leopard in here."*

No, she was staying right where she was. She'd just have to find some other way to convince everyone to trust her.

Uraza let out a kind of "you better" grumble-purr. She nudged Abeke's hand with her head again and then stalked gracefully away, lashing her tail. The wind sent ripples across her black-spotted golden fur.

"Everything all right?" Lenori said from behind her as Abeke stood up.

Abeke nodded. They'd stopped at Greenhaven only long enough to pick up Lenori and leave Maya – poor, devastated Maya. And then *Tellun's Pride* had sailed, with Lenori's visions driving them onward to Oceanus, where apparently a giant octopus really, really wanted a word with them.

"Couldn't we –" she blurted out, and then stopped herself.

"Couldn't we what?" Lenori asked gently.

"Couldn't we stop in Nilo?" Abeke asked. "Isn't there a Great Beast there? The lion, right? We could look for his talisman and then go to Oceanus, couldn't we?" *And maybe we could stop by my village . . . just to make sure they're all right.* She wondered if the rains had ever come. Or if the Conquerors had reached them first.

The Greencloak tipped her head sympathetically. "You miss your family. I understand; I miss mine too. And it's so much harder for you – at least mine are in Amaya, where the enemy has not yet penetrated."

"I don't know if I so much *miss* them," Abeke admitted. "But –"

"You're worried about them." The sea wind whipped through Lenori's long dark hair, and her rainbow ibis stood close within the shelter of her green cloak.

Abeke turned to look at the tangled green coastline again. "I wish they knew what I was doing, that I'm not with Zerif anymore. I wish I could help them figure out who to trust and who not to trust. I wish – I just wish I could see them again and be sure they're all right."

The beads in Lenori's bracelets clattered softly as the older woman touched Abeke's shoulder. "I believe they are," she said. "You are doing what must be done to save them. To save all of Erdas. You've been very brave."

Abeke wished she had Lenori's calm certainty about anything.

"I hope you will have a chance to see them again soon. But as for going to Nilo right now, I'm afraid it's too dangerous," Lenori went on. "All reports indicate that the Conquerors have overrun the whole continent, the way they've taken over Zhong."

All the more reason to go now, Abeke thought. *What about Father and Soama? What might the Conquerors have done to them?* She imagined them forced to drink Bile, joined to twisted and horrible animals, and controlled by the enemy. A shudder ran through her whole body.

"And it's not just the Conquerors," Tarik added, strolling over from the stern. Abeke jumped; she hadn't realized he'd been listening. "Cabaro the Lion is one of the most deadly of the Great Beasts. Before we approach him, the more talismans we have, the safer we'll be."

"Besides, Mulop is calling us," Lenori said, her face clouded as if she were watching something a great distance away. She held out her hand and her ibis leaned in close to her, staring at Abeke with its unsettling eyes. The rushing spray of the ocean below them nearly drowned out Lenori's quiet, musical voice as she murmured, "I have heard him in my dreams every night for a few weeks now. It starts with the sound of whales singing, and then the darkness around me turns blue, and I realize I'm underwater. The light is drifting down from far above, but it barely illuminates the cavern where I'm floating. And then a bubble spirals up past me, and another, and I realize they each contain a word, so I start trying to catch them, but they all pop as soon as I touch them. Except the words are left in blurred ink marks on my skin, so I can almost see a pattern, a message linking them all together."

"Almost?" Abeke asked.

"Visions are always a little cryptic," Lenori said. "Visions from Mulop, even more so. But what I can figure out says that he wishes to see the Four Fallen and their companions." She shook her head. "We shouldn't keep him waiting any longer than we have already. You *don't* say no to Mulop."

I wasn't going to say no, Abeke thought. *Just . . . right, sure, yes, be there soon, just give us a minute.*

"Especially since this is the first Great Beast who's reached out to us," Tarik observed. He gave Abeke a wry, sympathetic smile. "After our experience with Suka, we could use a more pleasant encounter, don't you agree? Somewhere with sunshine instead of frozen toes. Just imagine, a Great Beast who actually *wants* to see us. He may even be able to tell us more about what's happening. All the tales agree that Mulop is a powerful seer."

That all made sense, but Abeke had to admit she wasn't entirely convinced by Lenori's ambiguous vision. She heard footsteps on the deck and turned to see Rollan and Conor approaching. Briggan was in passive state—he was also not the greatest fan of sea travel – while Essix was aloft, soaring on the wind currents.

"This is the safest plan," Tarik added reassuringly. And then he went on, much less reassuringly, "The only part that worries me is that we will have to sail past Stetriol. I wish there were another way, but I'm afraid we'll just have to hope we can slip by unnoticed."

"Oh, good, hoping," Rollan commented. "That's always worked out well for us."

Tarik squinted at him.

"Don't you dare ask me again if I'm all right," Rollan said. He grinned in a way that was almost convincing, except that it didn't quite reach his eyes. "I've dealt with it. I've moved on. I am totally fine. Better than fine – I am now someone who can summon his spirit animal to passive mode! That's right, I'm awesome." He pulled open his shirt and angled his chest at the sky. "Wait for it. . . . Wait for it. . . ."

There was a pause. Nothing happened. Essix kept circling languidly far overhead, ignoring them all.

"Still waiting," Conor joked tentatively.

Rollan shrugged. "Doesn't matter. We have an understanding now. We totally get each other. Right, Essix?" he called.

The falcon shrieked, which might have meant, "Oh, put your shirt back on," but was at least better than the nonresponses Rollan used to get from her.

Abeke wondered if Rollan really was fine. She didn't see how he could be, after what had happened with his mother, Aidana, but he clearly didn't want to talk about it.

There had been a grand total of one conversation on the topic, which was all Rollan would allow. Everyone had noticed how quiet and shattered he was after the battle on the docks, but at first Abeke had thought it was because of losing the Crystal Polar Bear. After all, he'd been the one holding it when the walrus stole it away.

But then, two nights later, as they sailed for Greenhaven, Rollan had told them the whole story. How his mother had abandoned him as a child because her bond with her spirit animal was unstable, making her too dangerous to be around him. How she'd found peace with the Conquerors when she drank Bile, and her bond became manageable. How she'd tried to convince Rollan to join her — and then revealed the dark side of the Bile: Whoever drank it wound up under the control of the Conquerors.

Someone else had taken over her body, Rollan said. Something inhuman had looked out of her eyes and forced Aidana to try to kill her own son.

Abeke still felt shudders of horror whenever she thought about it. She couldn't imagine what that would feel like, to see someone she cared about taken over by a dark force. Or worse, to *be* that person, losing all control over your own body. Imagine attacking your own family and not being able to stop yourself. Was there anything worse?

Poor Rollan. Nobody knew if he'd ever see his mother again, or if she could ever truly *be* his mother again, now that the Bile controlled her.

But he didn't want to dwell on it. That was the conclusion of his story: He said he wanted no long heartfelt chats about it, no pitying looks, no sad faces, or else he'd have

Essix yell at them. What was done was done, and the truth was (he said) that he'd never really known his mother, so he doubted he'd miss her very much.

Abeke knew that was a lie, but it seemed to be a lie that Rollan needed to tell himself.

Ever since that night, he'd been acting like his old sarcastic self, with perhaps an extra note of swaggering now that Essix was finally willing to go into passive mode (occasionally).

Still, Abeke could tell that Tarik was worried about him. She thought they all were . . . but there was nothing they could do except give Rollan his space.

"Have you had any more visions?" Lenori asked Conor. "Has Mulop spoken to you?"

"Um," Conor said, "I wouldn't say *spoken*, exactly." He rubbed one hand through his blond hair, looking confused.

"I was just telling Abeke, visions from Mulop are always particularly strange," Lenori said, nodding. "What did you dream?"

"It started the same as the last one," Conor said. "I was floating in the air over a sea of islands—it looked like thousands of little green and white sheep scattered over the water. And then this dark cloud of ink started pouring into the water from the south, turning every island black as it touched them. And then—" He hesitated, glancing at Rollan.

"Go on," said Tarik. "He won't make fun of you."

"I absolutely will make fun of you," Rollan retorted. "But don't let that stop you."

"And then these long tentacles rose out of the ocean,"

Conor said, "and they started picking up the islands that were still green and throwing them at the black islands, knocking them back like a game of marbles. Which made the ink retreat too. And then the tentacles kind of pointed up at me, and then . . . they kind of waved. And then they went back under the water, and I woke up." He looked expectantly at Rollan.

"That's not fair," Rollan said. "That's barely hilarious at all."

"It doesn't give us a lot to go on," Lenori said, "but it's definitely Mulop trying to get our attention."

"I guess we are doing the right thing," Abeke said. Somehow, hearing it from Conor made her feel better about this plan. He shot her a smile, and she felt a twist of gratitude in her chest. *At least one of my friends is still treating me like a friend.*

"RRRRRRRRRRRRRRRRRRRRRRRRRRRRRRRRRRRR RRR."

A deep growl rolled across the deck, making all the hairs on Abeke's skin stand up. She whirled and saw Uraza poised in an attack crouch. The leopard's tail was lashing violently and her violet eyes, full of fury, were fixed on a perfectly harmless-looking seagull.

A seagull?

The gray-and-white bird sat on one of the crossbeams of the masts above the Greencloaks, too high up for even Uraza to leap and catch it. It looked no different from any of the other hundred seagulls that soared around them.

It clacked its beak and tilted its head, giving Uraza a black, beady-eyed stare.

"Uraza?" Abeke said. "What's wrong?"

The bird turned its head slowly back toward them. Its gaze passed over Abeke, and she felt a weird shiver down her spine. Then it stopped, staring intently at Conor.

"Looks like you have an admirer," Rollan joked. "See, Conor, this is why I keep telling you to bathe more. If you didn't smell so much like fish, you wouldn't—"

The seagull shrieked once, a piercing cry that sounded like its feathers were being ripped out.

And then it dove straight at Conor's face.

3

STORM

FEATHERS WERE SUDDENLY EVERYWHERE, SURROUNDING HIM, blocking out the sky and his friends and the air he had been breathing. Gray-and-white wings beat furiously at Conor's ears like blacksmith hammers trying to knock his brains out. An impossibly sharp beak jabbed at his face, at his vulnerable eyes, at his throat.

Conor let out a yell and stumbled back. The bird kept attacking, and he felt it painfully yank out several strands of his hair at once. He tried to cover his head, and the seagull instantly went for the pocket of his coat.

"The Granite Ram!" he heard Meilin yell, sounding very far away. "It's trying to steal one of our talismans!"

"It's a spirit animal!" Rollan shouted. "Working for the Conquerors!"

Conor could sense the others around him, trying to stop the gull, but it was relentless. He thrashed and rolled away, letting the bird pummel his back instead. Blows rained down on him. His hands clutched the stone ram in his pocket. He was *not* losing another talisman, not even if the seagull tried to peck out his eyes.

And then he heard a cry that he recognized as Essix's, and a moment later the seagull was suddenly gone from his back.

"Conor?" Abeke was beside him, crouching to check his face. "Are you all right?"

"Did it get the talisman?" Meilin demanded.

"No." He shook his head. The weight of the ram was still heavy in his pocket.

"Essix!" Rollan shouted. "Be careful!"

Conor sat up and looked to the sky. His clothes were torn and he could feel blood rolling down his face from at least two seagull-inflicted wounds, but he was more worried about where the bird was now.

High above them, he could see Essix and the seagull diving and snapping at each other.

"Don't let it get away," he gasped. "If it's a Bile-bonded creature, it could lead the Conquerors right to us."

Abeke sprang to her feet and whipped out her bow. In a moment she had an arrow notched and aimed, but then she hesitated.

"Shoot it!" Meilin yelled.

"I don't want to hit Essix!" Abeke shouted back.

Rollan cupped his hands around his mouth. "Essix!" he called. "Stop! Back off so we can shoot it!"

Essix screeched in response, but she dove and flapped away, leaving Abeke a clear shot.

Abeke fired the arrow, but it missed the seagull by a feather. Swiftly she drew and aimed again, but the second arrow was too late. The gull was already winging away into the clouds.

The falcon shrieked with what sounded like frustration, at least to Conor, who felt the same way. But he saw the look on Abeke's face, so as he climbed to his feet, he patted her shoulder. "It was an impossible shot," he said. "None of us could have made it either." He looked at Meilin for confirmation, but she just narrowed her eyes and didn't respond.

"But now the Conquerors will know where we are," Abeke said, her voice cracking. "That seagull could lead them right to us."

"They probably already know," Meilin said unhelpfully. "Since someone is passing them information, as you might remember."

"Meilin, it's not me!" Abeke protested. "I'm not the mole. I promise you can trust me!"

"*How?*" Meilin exploded. "How can any of us trust anyone anymore?" She clenched her fists as if she was trying to hold in her anger. "I *want* to, by all the Great Beasts, of course I do; I hate feeling angry and suspicious all the time, especially with you – I mean, with any of you," she added, but her gaze was fixed on Abeke. "I thought we were friends."

"We are," Abeke tried to interject. Conor wanted to jump in too, but he could see that Meilin was too upset to listen.

"But *someone* is the mole – someone has been leading the Conquerors straight to us over and over again," Meilin barreled on. "And no one seems to care and no one wants to talk about it, so fine, but what are we supposed to think when your Conqueror boyfriend keeps showing up just in time to steal talismans from us? That last battle—you realize that was the second time you were conveniently captured so you could be used as leverage against us?"

"He's not my boyfriend, and I would never ever do that on purpose," Abeke cried. "Shane is different from the others! I know we could reason with him if we got him away from the rest of the Conquerors. I swear, I was only trying to help us escape alive, because even if you don't believe it, Meilin, I really care about you. About all of you."

Meilin's shoulders dropped and she put her hands to her head, suddenly looking exhausted instead of confrontational. "I care about you too," she muttered after a moment, barely audible. "But who else—and how—I can't stop thinking about it. It's someone here. It's one of you, and it kills me—" She broke off, took a deep breath, and turned to Jhi. "Let's go get Conor some bandages." The two of them headed for the ladder that led below. Jhi walked close enough to brush Meilin's arm with her fur, a worried expression on the giant panda's face.

Abeke sighed.

Conor put his arm around her shoulder in a half hug. He knew how Meilin felt—every time he thought of Shane, he wanted to punch something, and he couldn't at all see what Abeke saw in him. But he knew what he himself saw in Abeke—courage, loyalty, and honor. He believed in her. He wasn't going to let any of the small voices of doubt reach into his brain and change that belief.

"Don't worry," he said to Abeke. "Meilin just prefers to have problems she can beat and stab and kick, instead of ones that circle around quietly haunting us. You know that. She's angry, but she'll come around once we – uh, once we . . ."

He trailed off. Once they figured out who the real mole was? How could that information be anything but devastating to all of them?

"Thanks," said Abeke, looking down at the rolling deck. "I think I need to – I'm just going below for a minute." She hurried away, brushing at her eyes, with Uraza close on her heels.

Conor wished he could have said something to make her feel better. They'd all been through so much together since Abeke first left the Conquerors and joined the Greencloaks. It didn't seem fair that suddenly she was back in the same corner of distrust and suspicion where she'd started out.

Well, she isn't. Not with me, anyhow.

He touched the tattoo on his arm where Briggan was dormant. He hadn't had time to call his spirit animal for help when the gull attacked; he hadn't even had a chance to think. He reached inside, calling for him now, and Briggan responded immediately, appearing next to Conor on the deck. The wolf looked Conor up and down and shot a dangerous glance at the remaining seagulls – a look that said, "Seagulls for dinner would be all right with me, if anyone else wants to try a stunt like that again."

Conor crouched and put an arm around Briggan, who started licking the wounds on Conor's face and hands.

After a moment, Conor shook himself, stood up, and headed over to Rollan and Tarik. The older Greencloak was leaning on the railing of the ship and looking back at the clouds where the seagull had vanished. Briggan stuck close to Conor's side with an alert, vigilant expression on his face.

"Are you all right? That was creepy," Rollan added as Conor nodded. He looked up at the other seagulls, several of which were perched on the mast crossbeams or along the sides of the ship. "How can we know which animals are working for the Conquerors?"

"There's no way to know unless they look unusually large or if they do something odd," Tarik said. "Uraza must have noticed the way that one was studying Conor." He glanced down at Conor, and without saying a word, Conor handed the Granite Ram over to the older Greencloak. It seemed safer if Tarik held on to it.

"I'd say we can expect more of that kind of thing," Tarik said, pocketing the talisman. "It's only going to get more dangerous the closer we are to Stetriol. We could be watched at all times."

Conor shivered. "Maybe that's how the mole is getting his information. Maybe it's not one of us—maybe it's some animal that's been following us."

"Aha," Rollan said. "I knew that boll weevil in my soup last night looked suspicious."

Conor smiled halfheartedly. It was an unsettling thought, but not as unsettling as the idea that one of their friends and fellow Greencloaks was working for the enemy.

As if he'd read his mind, Rollan added, "I've been try-ing to use this intuition thing to read everyone since we left Eura. And I swear, I'm only getting sincerity from everyone, including Abeke. I don't sense any deception or betrayal . . . it's weird." He kicked the railing, looking down at his feet. "Or maybe I'm missing something, the way I missed that Pia was lying when she gave me the compass."

He fell silent, and Conor guessed he was thinking of the darkness he hadn't seen inside Aidana either, until it was too late.

"Don't blame yourself," Tarik said. "For all we know, there is no mole and the Devourer just wants us to suspect each other."

Rollan nodded, but Conor could see that he didn't really believe it. The message from his mother had been pretty clear — someone among them was passing messages to the Conquerors. Somehow they had known exactly where the Greencloaks would be with the Crystal Polar Bear. Somehow they *always* knew.

It didn't make any sense, though. Conor's mind kept circling the options, leaving him more and more puzzled and worried.

Meilin hated the Conquerors for what they'd done to her father and her home — she'd never work with them. Abeke might be friendly with Shane, but Conor trusted her; she wasn't the kind of person who betrayed her friends, and she believed in the Greencloaks' cause. Rollan . . . maybe someone might think it was suspi-cious that Rollan still refused to join the Greencloaks. But if he was on the Devourer's side, he would have gone off with his mother, or at least he would have known about her and the Bile. Conor was sure Rollan hadn't been faking the pain that came with the story he'd told them.

So if it definitely wasn't any of them, who else could it be? Tarik or Lenori? Tarik was their guardian, their rock. Conor believed he would die to protect them if he had to. There was no reason for him to betray them. He didn't know as much about Lenori — and it had occurred to him that if she could receive visions from a great distance, perhaps she could send messages the same way. But that didn't feel true to what he knew about her either.

None of them made sense as the mole. But there was no one else it could be.

"I'll see if the whales can go any faster," Tarik said, straightening. "We're only a day away from the channel between Nilo and Stetriol, the most dangerous point of our journey. We need to travel as swiftly as we can. That seagull was only a harbinger of what's yet to come."

Conor felt a shiver travel down his spine.

Watched on all sides. Dangerously close to Stetriol. And divided among themselves, each of them looking at the others and wondering who the mole could be.

He had a strong, sinking feeling that this mission was going to end with loss and disaster.

"Are there any talismans that control the weather?" Rollan moaned from his hammock. The wind whistled outside, and furious waves thumped against the boards of the ship. The lanterns shook and swayed, flinging shadows jerkily around the room. Across the cabin, Abeke lay in her hammock with her arms over her face, silent. All of their animals were in passive state, even Essix.

"No," Meilin said from the floor, where she was calmly sharpening her knife. "Control the weather? Maybe a Great Beast could do that, but there's no talisman that could give that kind of power to a human. Obviously."

"Oh, sorry," Rollan said. "I forgot the talismans can only do normal, logical things like make a wolf the size of a house."

"Were you wondering if someone sent this storm to us?" Conor asked Rollan. He felt as green and seasick as the other boy looked. Their ship had been tossed and shaken and beaten and pummeled for days by hurricane-force winds and driving rain. At least they didn't have to worry about sails, which would have been destroyed immediately. The two massive rockback whales who towed the ship kept them steady and as close to their course as they could.

And yet the storm had still forced them from their planned path. Two days ago, during one of the few hours of calm, Conor had caught a glimpse of land off to the south. He knew it had to be Stetriol: home of the Devourer, prison of Kovo and Gerathon. That was as close as Conor ever wanted to come to that dark place.

"No, but that's a nice terrifying thought," Rollan said, answering Conor's question. He waved weakly at the dark portholes. "I just want to stop this rain already. You know, put on some albatross necklace and wave my fists at the clouds and poof, blue skies are back."

"There is no albatross among the Great Beasts," Meilin informed him.

"I *know*," he said. "Well, okay, possibly *my* fancy tutors never got to that, but the point is, I was just being metaphysical."

"Metaphorical," she corrected. "Actually, neither of those words makes sense there."

"Next time I throw up," he threatened, "it'll be into your soup bowl if you don't stop taking advantage of my illness to kick me while I'm down."

"Get anywhere near my soup bowl," Meilin said sweetly, "and you'll find out what getting kicked really feels like."

Conor decided it was time to get some fresh air.

The rocking of the ship seemed calmer than it had been for days, and the sound of the rain on the outside walls was no longer a relentless drumbeat. Perhaps the storm was finally passing.

He rolled himself cautiously out of his hammock, taking a moment to steady his legs before stepping over Meilin and heading for the passageway and the ladder to the upper deck. The sounds of Rollan and Meilin arguing faded behind him as he climbed up into the gray morning air.

Conor was right. The rain had slowed to a drizzly patter and the wind only tousled his hair cheerfully, as if it hadn't spent the last several days trying to hurl him bodily into the ocean. There were even glimpses of sky between the masses of gray clouds overhead, and up ahead he could see scattered sunbeams slanting down toward the distant islands.

Islands!

His heartbeat quickened and he dashed to the railing at the front of the ship.

He wasn't dreaming. Those were definitely islands on the horizon – more than one. It had to be the Hundred Isles!

Conor flew back down to their cabin. "We're here!" he cried excitedly. "The Hundred Isles! Come see!"

Rollan groaned mournfully, but Meilin sprang to her feet, and a moment later Abeke sat up to follow them.

As they reached the deck, Conor held out his arm and released Briggan. The wolf shook himself and sniffed the damp air, then turned to nudge Conor's hand. Conor scratched behind Briggan's ears, grinning.

"Almost there," he said to the wolf.

"But *not* actually there," Meilin pointed out grumpily. She glowered at the distant islands. "Being able to see them is not the same thing as arriving. I thought you meant we'd be on land in a few minutes."

"It's a relief to see land at all, though," Abeke said with a sigh. She stretched her arms up to the sky. "And to be able to breathe out here without drowning."

Essix shrieked in agreement behind them as Rollan released her into the sky. The falcon soared between the masts and up until she was just a small scratch against the clouds. Rollan staggered to the railing beside Conor and took a deep breath.

"See?" Conor said to him. "Don't you feel better already?"

Rollan stared out at the gray-blue sea in front of them. "Not exactly," he said. "Not if those are what I think they are." He pointed at a few dots far ahead on the water; Conor hadn't even noticed them before.

"Show-off," Meilin said. She started tying her hair back. "All right, what do your falcon-enhanced eyes see?"

"Tarik!" Rollan shouted urgently, whipping around. "Tarik!"

Tarik and his otter, Lumeo, came bounding across the deck toward them. "What is it?"

Rollan pointed at the dots. "Ships. Conquerors, I'm sure of it."

Tarik took out a spyglass and studied the ocean for a long moment. "Blocking our path to the Hundred Isles," he said finally, his knuckles whitening as he gripped the telescope. "I should have expected this."

"Maybe that seagull . . ." Abeke started.

"They'd have been waiting for us regardless," Conor said. "They knew we'd have to come looking for Mulop eventually."

"We'll have to fight our way past them," Tarik said grimly.

"Oh, hooray," Rollan said, resting his elbows on the railing and dropping his head into his hands.

Tarik strode off to warn the sailors, and soon the ship was bustling with activity as everyone prepared for a sea battle.

Until the time came to fight, there was nothing Conor and his friends could do except watch the ships coming closer and closer. It felt to Conor exactly like the time a fire had raged through his village, inexorably consuming everything in its path. He'd only been three years old, but it was one of his earliest memories, particularly that feeling of helpless dread . . . knowing something awful was coming for you, and that there was nothing you could do about it.

Conor twisted his staff in his hands and touched the ax at his belt. He wished he had a bow like Abeke's instead. His weapons would be most useful at close range – but if the Conquerors got close enough for that, they'd be on the ship, and that . . . would be very bad.

"Only six ships," Meilin said. Her jaw was set and her eyes flashed as though she was assessing the distances, wind direction, and weaknesses of their attackers. "And our whales swim faster than they can sail. If we can just get past them, we should be able to escape into the islands."

If . . . Conor thought. The odds were six to one, and it looked like the ships were swarming with warriors and animals. He remembered their last battle and how badly they'd been outnumbered. This time there was no Maya to set all their enemies on fire.

Abeke leaned precariously over the railing, peering down at the whales. "What are those?" she asked, pointing.

Conor felt a stab of fear go through him as he recognized the sharp triangular fins slicing through the water. "Sharks," he said just as Abeke gasped with recognition too.

"It's all right," Meilin said uneasily. "They can't hurt us as long as we don't go in the water."

"Guess I'll postpone my usual morning swim, then,"

Rollan said, but even his wisecracking sounded tense, and his eyes were worried as they all watched the sharks draw closer and closer.

The creatures were huge, with cruel teeth big and scary enough to see all the way from the deck of the ship. Their unblinking eyes seemed to glare up at the Greencloaks. These were clearly Bile-enhanced sharks, hideously oversized after being forced to drink the evil liquid – and horribly dangerous.

But if they couldn't attack the people on the ship, then surely there was nothing to worry about. . . .

"The whales!" he cried, suddenly figuring out the plan. "They're going to hurt the whales!"

The first shark had already reached the long, mottled gray-and-black side of one of the rockback whales. Conor watched in horror as it attacked, ripping its fierce teeth into the innocent whale's flesh.

The rockback whale let out a cry of pain that echoed eerily, like a stone mountain calling out for help. Its partner called back, long and low and tragic, but there was nothing it could do to help. More sharks were already descending, at least six to each whale. Conor could see blood seeping from the first wounds. He knew the blood would attract even more sharks, regular ones. As vast as they were, the whales were not fighters, and they had no protection against the vicious predators. They couldn't even submerge and hide in the deep; if they went under, they'd drag the ship down with them.

"Can you shoot them?" he asked Abeke, turning to

see that she already had her bow drawn. Uraza stood next to her, growling and lashing her tail.

Abeke bit her lip, concentrating, and then fired. The arrow plunged into the nearest shark and it writhed angrily for a moment before a second arrow skewered its eye. As it sank below the water, Conor felt a weird twinge of pity for it. It had been living its normal life as a normal shark until someone came along, captured it, and forced Bile down its throat to change it into an enormous, rage-filled monster. Then again, normal sharks weren't exactly pleasant either.

Abeke drew her bow again, but the sharks had all moved farther away, closer to the whales' heads, out of range. She fired anyway, but her arrow vanished harmlessly into the sea.

She swore, brushing away tears, and reached for another arrow.

"Maybe you should save those for the Conquerors," Conor said softly. He nodded at the ships that were now sailing into a blockade around them.

"But those poor whales," Abeke said. "They don't deserve this."

He agreed with her. He felt sick at the sight of the majestic, gentle rockbacks under attack. But there was nothing he could do to protect them except fight off the enemy. Boats full of Conquerors and their animals were already rowing toward them. Grappling hooks shot onto the deck of *Tellun's Pride*, slithering back to catch on the railings. Conor hefted his staff and turned to join Tarik and the other sailors.

"Meilin!" Rollan yelled suddenly from behind him. "What are you *doing*?"

Conor looked back and saw that Meilin had grabbed a spear from a nearby sailor and vaulted onto the railing at the bow of the ship. With a swift, graceful movement, she crouched—and vanished over the side.

4

SHARKS

SALT SPRAY PELTED MEILIN'S FACE AS SHE SWUNG FROM ONE of the ropes that connected the ship to the rockback whales. Dark water yawned far below her, eager to swallow her up if the sharks didn't get her first. She heaved her feet up to the rope and wrapped them around, and then she started pulling herself down toward the whales, hand over hand. The sharp edges of the rope cut into her palms in a million places, but she kept going, ignoring the shouts of her friends back on the ship.

Someone had to help the whales, and they certainly couldn't do it from up there.

The rope jounced and swung precariously as she dipped toward the restless ocean. Her heart skipped a beat as one of the shark fins sliced through the water right below her.

Nope. Don't even think about it. I refuse to be eaten by sharks.

Her shoulders were yelling with agony by the time she glanced down and finally saw the rocky slope of the whale's back below her. Taking a deep breath, she unhooked her legs and dropped into a crouch on top of the whale. The rope continued past overhead, connecting with a kind of harness near the whale's mouth.

Nothing to panic about. It's like walking on a beach, she told herself. A beach strewn with rocks and boulders . . . which happened to be moving very quickly . . . and was incredibly wet and slippery underfoot . . . oh, and PS, also had *deadly sharks* snapping and lunging only a few feet away.

The whale beneath her let out another mournful bellow of pain. The vibrations echoed through Meilin's bones and made her heart ache. She placed her open hand on the whale's back, in a clear spot between the rocks.

"It's all right," she whispered. "I won't let them hurt you anymore."

Meilin rose, took a step, and immediately slipped, cracking her knee on one of the rocks jutting out of the whale's back. She let out a hiss of pain and then stood again, gritting her teeth. After a moment she figured out how to balance and how to grip the slick surface with her boots. She edged forward, pulling out the spear she'd strapped to her back.

She counted seven sharks around this whale, but it seemed like more from the way they thrashed and churned the water. Bloody froth splashed up the sides of the whale and across Meilin's boots. The wind yanked fiercely at her cloak and hair, still heavy with rain.

One of the sharks spotted Meilin and suddenly lunged up onto the whale, whipping its tail back and forth and smashing its teeth together only inches away from her legs. Meilin stumbled back but managed to stay upright. *Do not fall. Most importantly: Do not fall into the water.* She'd be ripped apart in seconds if that happened. *Definitely do not think about that.*

With a yell of anger, she lifted the spear and drove it into the shark's open mouth. A burst of energy flooded her as she did, and the point of the spear came stabbing out the top of the shark's head. It tried once to gnash its teeth again, then flopped sideways, dead.

Meilin yanked the spear free — it took a few tries; it was harder coming out than going in — and kicked the shark until its momentum carried it sliding down the side of the whale into the ocean. It disappeared below the surface in a flurry of red bubbles.

Encouraged, she darted along the whale's back to the next shark, which had its teeth firmly embedded in the side of the whale and was thrashing as if trying to rip out as big a piece as possible. Meilin paused above it, and for one chilling moment the shark's eye stared right into hers. Then she plunged the spear straight through that eye with skill-ful accuracy.

The shark convulsed powerfully, nearly jerking Meilin right into the ocean. She fell forward and had to scramble with her legs and one hand to find a grip on the rocky whale, while clutching the spear with her other hand. For a long, awful moment, she thought she was going to be dragged into that seething mass of sharks, and she nearly let go of the spear.

But at last the shark stopped moving, and she was able

to kick it off the spear point into the water.

The whale made another wounded sound and Meilin saw three sharks circle around and head straight toward her, faster than any animal should be able to swim. Their teeth gleamed sharply, even below the water.

She clambered back up to the middle of the whale's back and stood up again, facing the sharks with her spear held high. From here she could see all the spots where blood was pouring from twenty different wounds. The whale was slowing down. It was vast enough that one shark bite couldn't do too much damage – but this many injuries . . .

Reluctantly, she held out her arm, and a moment later, Jhi appeared beside her on the whale's back.

The panda's paws immediately slipped on the wet surface and she sprawled out like an ungainly puppy.

"Hruff!" she grunted, giving Meilin a startled look.

"I know," Meilin said. "We're on a whale. Sorry about that. Is there anything you can do to help it?" She pointed to the multiple injuries.

Jhi tried to stand up, scrabbled her paws frantically for a moment, and then collapsed onto her back.

"Hruumf," she observed at the sky.

"Well, see what you can do," Meilin said impatiently. "And don't fall in the water."

She hurried away from the panda, heading for the next shark. She could feel Jhi's energy filling her, slowing time down so that she could see every step to take and move faster than she could on her own. Filled with that dreamlike peace, she swung her spear at another shark and impaled it through the side, then flung it out into the water. A fourth shark lunged up onto the whale, snapping at her boots, and Meilin dispatched it swiftly.

The next shark saw her coming and dove, sinking its teeth into the whale underwater, too far down for Meilin to reach it with her spear. She stopped, frustrated, and saw the next closest shark do the same thing. There was a lot of whale underwater, and no way for her to get there to protect its vulnerable underbelly.

She looked back at Jhi. The panda was crouched low with her paws splayed out, braced against the biggest rocks she could find. Her head stretched toward the closest shark bite and her nose twitched helplessly. Her furry black-and-white rump stuck up in the air.

Meilin rolled her eyes and sighed. *Oh, Jhi. That's what I get for bringing a panda to a shark fight. A leopard or a falcon could at least do some damage.* But she also, unexpectedly, felt a stab of sympathy for the giant panda. The top of a rockback whale was clearly no place for her, and yet Jhi was trying her best to do as Meilin had asked. But how could anyone heal the whales in a situation like this, even a Great Beast?

Beyond her, Meilin could see the *Tellun's Pride* – and she could see the Conquerors swarming up its sides. On deck, Rollan and Tarik were each grappling with opponents who were bigger and burlier than they were, while Abeke leaned over the side, shooting at the ones still climbing aboard. *Where's Conor?* She finally spotted him, whacking his ax into one of the ropes the Conquerors were using to shimmy over the railing.

Maybe that's what we have to do, she realized, looking up at the whale's harness. *If we cut the whales free, they can submerge and escape the sharks.*

But if they did that, the ship would have no chance of escaping the Conquerors. The speed of the whales was their only advantage, if they could just break free and use it. Without the whales, they'd be dead in the water until they got the sails up . . . if they could even do that in the middle of a battle . . . and then they'd be as slow as the ships chasing them.

She looked down again at the sad, wounded whales. None of that mattered; cutting them free was what she had to do. She'd never be able to fight off all these sharks by herself, especially since she could see even more menacing fins slicing through the dark water now, drawn by all the blood.

Meilin swore and darted back toward Jhi. The panda blinked her soft silver eyes at Meilin, who held out her arm. Jhi glanced woefully at the whale's injuries and then vanished into the tattoo again.

Once I get back on ship, I can cut the whales free and then help fight off the Conquerors. Maybe with my help, we can drive them off, Meilin thought. She didn't really believe it.

She turned to find a spot where she could jump up to the ropes – and then she saw a girl in the water.

Meilin blinked, and the girl was gone.

What?

Surely that was impossible. A girl in the water, out here?

Then she saw her again — a flash of dark hair and brown arms, out beyond the sharks.

Is she swimming? Here? Now?

Did she need to be rescued?

The girl's head rose out of the water and Meilin realized that she was riding something — a dolphin — just as they submerged again.

Was she a Conqueror? A dolphin didn't seem like the kind of animal a Conqueror would choose to bond with, but maybe.

She squinted through the haze of sea spray and light rain until the girl came up again. Now Meilin could see that she was wearing a long green cloak woven from seaweed. The girl lifted both arms in the air and waved.

Is she waving at me?

Meilin raised her arm to wave back — and then she spotted movement on the closest islands.

It looked like almost a hundred people were suddenly hurrying down onto the beaches and launching long war canoes. The boats leaped into the water and flew toward the battling ships.

Oh! Meilin realized. *She was signaling them.* The native islanders were joining the fight — coming to help the Greencloaks, Meilin guessed. Well, she hoped.

She looked up at her friends struggling on the deck of the ship.

Would they reach the ship in time?

Would it be enough to save the whales?

5

KALANI

"FOOLISH STUPID CRAZY STUPID LUNATIC BRAINLESS—" ROLLAN yelled, swinging his short sword furiously at the Conqueror in front of him.

"What did you call me?!" the burly man bellowed, pausing his attack for a moment to glare down at Rollan.

"I'm not talking about you!" Rollan hollered, then kicked the man as hard as he could in the midsection—a move he'd learned on the streets, not in any Greencloak training session. With a muffled "Oof!" the man staggered backward and tumbled over the railing into the sea.

Rollan could barely feel the flash of triumph beneath all his worries. What was Meilin *thinking*? Running around on top of whales! In the middle of the ocean! Smack in the center of a deadly shark attack! She could be the most brilliant and graceful warrior Zhong had ever produced (he suspected she was), and that would *still* be the worst idea of all time.

He caught a glimpse of her far below, wielding a spear against a shark at least twice her size, before another Conqueror leaped onto the deck and sent a knockout punch flying toward his face.

Rollan ducked in the nick of time and stabbed his knife up into the man's bicep. At the same moment, Essix hurtled out of the sky and seized something off the attacker's shoulder. As she flew up again, Rollan realized it was a tarantula, writhing and flailing in the falcon's claws. The Conqueror's spirit animal, no doubt. Rollan shuddered. If those hairy legs had reached him . . .

"Thank you!" he shouted up at Essix. She sank her talons into the tarantula and flung it into the deep water below.

The Conqueror bellowed with rage and came for Rollan. His face was contorted with fury, and blood dripped down his arm.

Rollan tried to duck away again, but meaty hands knocked his knife to the deck, wrapped around his windpipe, and began to choke him.

As he gasped for breath, his mother's face flashed in his mind. But it wasn't really Aidana's face—not with those yellow, inhuman eyes, or the snarling expression. He remembered her fingers around his neck. He'd stared at the bruises in the mirror for weeks afterward.

That was the Bile, a voice yelled in his head. *She was being controlled by something evil.*

He saw a flash of green as Tarik whirled toward him. In a moment, the hands were gone from his neck; in another moment, the tarantula-less Conqueror was spiraling down toward the growing crowd of waiting sharks.

"Are you all right?" Tarik called.

Rollan nodded, not sure he could speak. He didn't think he'd even get to catch his breath before someone else attacked.

But then he heard shouts in another language. And splashes. And the thunk-thunk of arrows hitting the side of the ship – along with shrieks from Conquerors who were in the way of those arrows.

Tarik fought his way to the railing with Rollan right behind him.

"Who's that?" Rollan asked. Below them was a whole armada of war canoes, with brightly painted colors glowing warmly in the sunlight. Green-tattooed warriors grappled with Conquerors, preventing them from reaching the *Tellun's Pride*. Others were visible in the water, riding dolphins or orcas, driving away the sharks.

Tarik grinned at him. "Reinforcements. Allies. A welcoming committee. Whatever you want to call them!"

They turned back to the fight with renewed vigor, and soon there were no Conquerors left on the deck of the ship. Down in the water, the rockback whales were moving again, as swiftly as they could, leaving the wreckage of the Conquerors' blockade behind them. They also left a heart-wrenching trail of blood through the bright green and blue water, but a battalion of swimmers and sea creatures now surrounded and protected them from any more sharks, Bile-enhanced or otherwise.

Rollan kept his gaze on Meilin, who rode crouched on

top of a rockback whale. Her dark hair flew back in the wind and her cloak whipped around her shoulders. Her pale hands rested lightly on the whale's surface, as if she was taking its pulse. She didn't look up at him or the others on the ship. All of her energy seemed to be focused on the whales.

The sun broke through the clouds as they reached the islands. They were guided into a peaceful lagoon with water as blue as Briggan's eyes, sheltered by tall island cliffs on either side and deep enough for the whales to swim comfortably. As soon as the whales came to a stop, they were mobbed by islanders in smaller canoes, all carrying baskets of something green.

Rollan saw Meilin stand up. A moment later, Jhi appeared beside her, wobbling clumsily. Meilin gently put one hand on Jhi's head and leaned in as if she was listening. Then she started pointing to the shark bites and barking orders at everyone swimming or paddling around the whales.

"Let's go," Tarik said, nudging Rollan.

One of the ship's rowboats took them to shore. Rollan thought he had never been so happy to set foot on land before. The weeks of seasickness, the sudden battle, his worries about Meilin – all vanished in an instant as his boots touched solid ground. He even, for the first time in weeks, managed to push his mother's darkness out of his head. With a whoop, he did a cartwheel in the sand and fell over.

Abeke collapsed onto the beach beside him. Conor looked like he wanted to as well, but Briggan was leaping around him, yipping joyfully. With a grin, Conor picked up a stick and threw it. Briggan raced off after it, but got distracted halfway there by Lumeo the otter, who was jumping in the waves. The two spirit animals romped playfully around each other, scattering sand in all directions. Conor started laughing, and Tarik grinned down at him.

"What is that face?" Abeke said to Uraza. "I thought you'd be thrilled to be back on land." The big leopard was sitting beside her, shaking one front paw and then the other. Uraza paused and gave Abeke a disapproving look. She twitched her whiskers and sniffed her paw again, then flicked it at Abeke. A shower of damp sand came off her fur.

"Oh," Abeke said, patting her sympathetically. "It's just sand. It's not that bad, is it?"

Uraza turned up her nose, flicked her tail, and stalked off toward the jungle of dark green trees visible at the top of the beach.

"I hope the rockbacks are all right," Lenori said, twisting her long hair into a braid as she stared out at the water. Her bare feet sank into the sand and the waves rippled over and around the hollows they left. "Every time I think I've seen the worst of what the Conquerors will do, some new horror surprises me. Those whales are innocent, gentle creatures, not even spirit animals. Such brutality . . . such cruelty . . ." She stopped and took a deep breath. Lines of pain were etched in her face, as if she'd suffered along with the whales.

"They will heal," Tarik reassured her. "We'll make sure of that. They may be gentle, but they are also strong."

"I'd like to go out there and check on them," Lenori

said. "Ah, here comes a canoe now." She waved.

Rollan pivoted to look out at the whales and saw the canoe that was approaching – a canoe with Meilin inside. It slid onto the beach with a whooshing crunch sound.

"I can't believe you!" he exploded at her before her feet had even touched the ground. "You are the most head-strong, stubborn, brainless person I've ever met!"

"Oh, really?" Meilin snapped back. "Then let me intro-duce you to this guy I know. His name is Rollan." She strode past him, nodding at the others.

Lenori stopped her, murmured something that sounded like "thank you" in Meilin's ear, and then hurried down to climb into the canoe. Her ibis stepped majestically in behind her and stood like a long, thin statue in the bow of the boat. Two rowers returned the canoe to the bustle of activity around the rockbacks.

"Will the whales be all right?" Abeke asked Meilin, scrambling to her feet.

"I think so," Meilin said. "It seems like they're in good hands." She released Jhi, who gave a little jump when her paws touched the sand. The panda turned in a circle, looked thoughtful for a moment, then slowly lay down and started rolling on her back. Her huge paws flopped goof-ily from side to side. Meilin raised an eyebrow at her, but didn't say anything.

"That was amazing, what you did," Conor said to Meilin in an awestruck voice. "Those poor whales."

"Don't encourage her," Rollan said. "She's lucky she's not shark chow right now."

"You still could be shark chow if you like," Meilin said,

waving one hand at the ocean. "I bet I could throw you pretty far."

"*One* wrong step!" he yelled. "And then you'd be all eaten by sharks and where would we be? What would we do without—" *What would I do if something happened to Meilin?* "Without—uh, without Jhi? Did you even think of how much danger she was in?"

Something that might possibly have been actual contrition flashed across Meilin's face, but before she could respond, a splash from the sea distracted them all.

Rollan turned and saw a girl walking out of the waves. She was probably about sixteen years old and very tall—taller than Tarik, even. Her long black hair was wet and woven in a braid down her back, and her brown eyes were large and serious. Green stone earrings pierced her earlobes and a silver piercing that looked a little like a fishhook glittered from one eyebrow.

On her right shoulder, a black dolphin tattoo stood out in a sea of green whorls and patterns; green tattoos covered her arms from shoulder to wrist and continued across her collarbone. But they weren't like Finn's tattoos, hiding his spirit animal. Her dolphin was the centerpiece that everything swirled around.

"Welcome to the Hundred Isles," she said, wringing seawater out of her braid. "I am Kalani." Two islanders ran up as Kalani took off her dripping green seaweed cloak; one took it from her with careful ceremony, while the other handed her a new, dry green cloak. It wasn't quite like Tarik's and Lenori's cloaks, though. This one appeared to be made out of hundreds of bright green feathers.

She settled it around her shoulders and held her hand out to shake Tarik's. "I am so sorry we did not come to your aid sooner. We try to stay out of the Conquerors' sight, and we weren't sure you were Greencloaks. Not until we saw you trying to rescue the rockback whales." Kalani smiled at Meilin. "In other parts of the world, creatures of the sea are not treated with the same compassion and respect as they are here. But your bravery and kindness toward the whales were clear as day. We knew you must have a great love for all animals if you would risk your life for them — and we knew that, whether you were Greencloaks or not, we had to help you."

"Ha-HA," Meilin said to Rollan, tossing her head. "Compassion and respect! So THERE."

He rolled his eyes at her. "Have some compassion and respect for my nerves next time," he muttered.

"We are in your debt," Tarik said to Kalani. "I'm not sure what would have happened if you hadn't come to our rescue." He tilted his head at her cloak. "We knew there were Greencloaks here, but there wasn't time to send a message that we were coming — not one that we could trust wouldn't be intercepted, in any case."

"Our isles are overrun by enemies at the moment," Kalani said. "It often feels like venomous jellyfish tentacles are wrapping tighter and tighter around us. But Greencloaks survive, and we protect our corner of Erdas as best we can."

The islander who had brought her cloak spoke up. "Queen Kalani will always keep us safe. She has the ferocity of her mother and the wisdom of her father, may the ocean watch over their souls."

Tarik bowed, low and quickly, so Rollan guessed he was the only one who'd caught the look of surprise on their guardian's face. "Apologies, Your Majesty. I did not know . . . I had not heard that the former king and queen . . ."

"It was a night attack," Kalani said, "only a few months ago." She fingered one of the green feathers jutting out of her cloak, her face shadowed with grief. "My parents were killed and the Conquerors took my two older brothers, we assume to enslave them." Her dark eyes flicked up and caught Rollan's, and he saw a hard warrior inside the dolphin girl. He could imagine her running a gang of her own on the streets of Concorba, if she'd been born into a life like his. To tell the truth, he could imagine her eventually running the whole city.

"For some reason, it did not occur to them to try to take me," Kalani said, emphasizing the word *try*. "So now I am queen. And my plan is to show them they overlooked the most dangerous member of the family." She held out her hands, and the way she moved her arms made it look as though her tattoos were rippling like water.

Rollan glanced sideways and saw the admiring look on Meilin's face. A warrior queen, driven to avenge her parents' death — that was Meilin's kind of person, all right. As long as Kalani and Meilin were on the Greencloaks' side, Rollan figured the Devourer had better watch out.

"You look like you've come a long way," Kalani observed, studying each of them. "Much like ancient sea turtles after a lengthy journey. Why are you here?"

Rollan's first instinct was to lie, but he was distracted by the startling news that he looked like an ancient sea turtle and didn't speak fast enough. In any case, his instinct was no match for Conor's, which was always to blurt out the truth.

"We're looking for Mulop." Conor peered out at the water, then back at the tall cliffs of the island, running one hand through his disheveled blond hair. "It's really important that we speak to him."

"You can't be serious. Nobody speaks to Mulop," Kalani said, raising her eyebrows. "Do you regularly converse with Great Beasts in your part of the world?"

"Not exactly," Conor said. "Well, 'regularly' would be overstating it, anyway."

She gave him a puzzled look. "We revere Mulop, but no one has seen him in probably hundreds of years. He may as well live in the darkest cavern of the deepest part of the ocean."

"'May as well'?" Rollan echoed. "Does that mean you know where he actually is?"

Kalani's face clouded and she sighed.

"There's only one person who knows how to find Mulop," she said. "That knowledge has been preserved and passed down, from wise man to wise woman to our present wise man. But he's . . . well, he's unusual."

"Unusual how?" Rollan asked. "Believe me, we've met with plenty of unusual so far. Rhinoceros riders, underground cities of ice, Conor in a skirt — don't get me started."

The green feathers on her cloak rippled as Kalani shook her head. "I can't promise anything, but I'll take you to him," she offered. "Let's see if he will help you."

6

TANGAROA

ABEKE SHIVERED AS SHE FOLLOWED KALANI THROUGH THE flourishing jungle. Trees crowded around them and vines hung with bright red flowers snaked down from the branches to suddenly wind around their feet on every other step. Strange birds shrieked and whistled in the trees. Once, a face peering through the leaves made her jump, before she realized it was just a monkey.

Even "just a monkey" could be working for the Conquerors, though, she thought nervously.

That wasn't the only thing making her anxious. This jungle reminded her of another island – far away, in the Gulf of Amaya, where she had stayed with Shane back before she'd joined the Greencloaks. *Before I knew what the Conquerors were really like.*

It was on an island just like this where she and Uraza had spied on a group of men testing out the Bile on innocent animals. She'd seen them turn an ordinary rat and a well-behaved dog into a pair of horrible monsters, oversized and violent and nasty. Here, in another overgrown, humid jungle, it was hard not to think of that gigantic dog chasing her, of that terrifying flight through trees very much like these ones.

Abeke felt Uraza's fur brushing her fingers and looked down to find the leopard padding close to her side. Maybe Uraza was reliving the same memories.

"It's really hot," Rollan complained.

"At least you're not wearing a cloak," Meilin said pointedly, and he fell silent. Rollan was still the only one of all of them who'd refused to accept the green mantle of the Greencloaks. Abeke wasn't sure what he was waiting for. He'd proven his loyalty. He could have gone with his mother back on the docks of that town in Northern Eura, but he'd stayed with them instead.

Kalani stopped and held up one hand. Everyone paused behind her, waiting. Abeke tilted her head and listened. A large blue butterfly with black spots drifted off a nearby tree and landed briefly in Kalani's hair, its color vibrant and bright against the dark strands.

"Ah ha ha ha!" a voice shouted somewhere up ahead of them. "That was a good one, Ngaio! I might never have looked there if you hadn't sneezed. My turn to hide!"

Kalani shook her head, sending the butterfly fluttering away, and started moving again. Abeke and Conor exchanged mystified glances. Beside Conor, Briggan had his nose to the ground, sniffing vigorously at the layers of rotting vegetation underfoot. Essix was somewhere high above them, hidden by the thick canopy of treetops, and Jhi ambled slowly at the back. Up by Kalani, Tarik had

Lumeo curled around his shoulders, and he kept turning to make sure they were all still there.

They clambered over an enormous fallen tree with ridged bark that made perfect footholds. Something with way too many legs hissed at Abeke and scuttled away into the underbrush. Sweat rolled down her face and back. She almost missed the freezing wind and icy, insect-free snow of Arctica—but not really.

Kalani stopped again in a clearing. Abeke's hunter's eyes could tell that someone had been here recently, trampling light footprints in the fallen leaves. She touched Uraza's neck fur again and felt a surge of heightened awareness. Now she could see the small broken leaf stems on the tree across from her, along with two spots on the trunk where trails of ants were detouring around squashed insects. Whoever had been here hadn't run off into the jungle. He'd gone *up*.

She tilted her head back, and this time the face looking back at her was no monkey. He grinned like a monkey and thumbed his nose at her, but that was unmistakably the face of an old man, perhaps sixty years old or more.

"Hoy, Kalani!" he called down. "You're ruining our game!"

There was a cry of glee off in the trees, followed by crashing sounds as something came swinging through the branches toward them. Long hairy arms covered in bright orange fur circled the man's neck, hugging him tight.

"See?" the old man said to Kalani half-accusingly, half-teasingly. "It's very hard to play hide-and-seek with a whole crowd of visitors staring up at your magnificent hiding spot."

"This is Tangaroa," Kalani said to Abeke and the others.

"And this is Ngaio," Tangaroa added proudly, jumping down to the ground. It was a fairly long distance, but he landed with a bounce. Abeke guessed that was a skill sharpened by his spirit animal.

Wrapped around his back was a large, beaming orangutan. A bright red hibiscus flower was tucked behind one of her ears. She waved and showed them all her teeth. Abeke was struck by how similar Tangaroa's and Ngaio's expressions were, as if they'd spent a whole lot of time together. Tangaroa's wispy white hair even stuck up in tufts much like Ngaio's fur.

"My friends need your help," Kalani said. "They're looking for Mulop."

"Mulop!" Tangaroa shouted. Ngaio leaped off his back and they both began capering madly around the clearing as if locusts were crawling all over them. "Mulop, Mulop, Mulop!" Tangaroa sang. Ngaio echoed him with grunts, and they both giggled hysterically.

Next to Abeke, Uraza growled. "Shh," Abeke whispered, smoothing the leopard's fur.

Tangaroa stopped suddenly and pointed straight at Abeke and Uraza. "That is a leopard," he said.

"Eeeeee!" Ngaio shrieked in agreement.

"Yes," Kalani said. "But not just any leopard — it's Uraza, reborn."

"I don't care if it's the Emperor of Zhong," said Tangaroa. "*We* don't like leopards." He sat down abruptly and turned up his nose. Ngaio climbed into his lap, and Tangaroa absently began combing out her tangled fur with his fingers.

"I'm sorry," Abeke said, not sure what she was apologizing for.

"You don't have to apologize for your spirit animal," Kalani said. "I think someone else here should be sorry for his rudeness, though." She gave Tangaroa a hard stare. "Just because he lives on his own in the forest doesn't mean he gets to have the manners of a disagreeable lobster."

"Mulop," Tangaroa mumbled into Ngaio's ear. "Think he'll be pleased to see them?"

Ngaio answered by baring her teeth at Uraza.

"Me neither," said the old man.

"Yes, he will," Conor said eagerly. "He sent us a dream message. He wants to see us — it's really important that we find him."

"The safety of Erdas depends on it," Tarik added.

"Then why didn't *he* tell you where he is?" Tangaroa asked shrewdly. He waved his hands, startling an orange-spotted lizard into darting under a rock. "HMMMMM?"

"Probably because he expected you to help them," Kalani said. "Instead of acting like an embarrassing mule-headed pig's snout."

Abeke squashed the giggles that were threatening to burst out of her.

"Ooo, good one," Rollan murmured. "I should write that down."

Tangaroa tapped his teeth, unfazed by the insult. "I *might* be able to do that. But would it be *wise*? Is that what a *wise* man would do? Would a *wise* man have anything to say to a leopard or anyone who travels with leopards? When trusted with a sacred knowledge of this sort, should one hand it out *willy-nilly*, so to speak, to anyone who happens to wear a green cloak? Assuming one remembers said sacred knowledge, of course." He tapped his head. "The old coconut may have a few cracks in it these days."

Is he really that bothered by leopards? Abeke wondered. *Will he refuse to help us just because Uraza is here?*

"Do you know how to find him or not?" Meilin demanded.

"Of course I know," said the old man. "More or less. That is, I know how to call the Kingray, who can take you to him." He scratched the back of his head. "If I remember that right. It's been a while. Nobody's called on Mulop in many years. Ngaio! Quick, to our thinking positions!"

Ngaio leaped off his lap and somersaulted into a headstand. Tangaroa did the same, ending up with his wizened bare feet in the air. They both scrunched their faces into absurd expressions of deep thought.

There was a long pause.

"Maybe we should come back later," Kalani said.

"There's no time for that," Meilin snapped. "Is this lunatic really the only person in all the Hundred Isles who can guide us to Mulop?"

"Meilin," Tarik said with a note of reproof.

"Indeed I am," said Tangaroa serenely, keeping his eyes closed.

Kalani tossed her braid back and looked down at

Meilin. "This lunatic is nearly as old as a whale king. Show a little respect for your elders," she said. She crouched beside Tangaroa's upside-down head. "Grandfather. For the safety of the Hundred Isles and all our people, and indeed for the protection of Erdas itself, I'm afraid I must order you to help these Greencloaks."

"Grandfather?" Conor whispered.

"Whoops," Rollan said with a smirk, elbowing Meilin in the ribs. She shot him a glare.

Tangaroa and his orangutan sprang to their feet and swept their arms out in matching bows toward Kalani. Abeke thought they looked rather like giant, ridiculous birds.

"Your wish is my command," he said, "as my grand-daughter and as my queen. Ah, but wait! Mulop is revered by all the tribes. He is the sacred and beloved Great Beast for all of Oceanus. Shouldn't I respect his aura of mystery? His love of privacy? Besides, *how* do I know we can trust these alleged Greencloaks?"

Ngaio lifted her arms and gave them all a look that said: "Well? How can he? What can anyone do, I mean, right?"

Kalani rubbed her forehead, looking as if she would rather negotiate with fire ants than continue this conversation.

"Ask us anything," Abeke jumped in. "We only want to protect Erdas, and to do that we need to see Mulop. We're the good guys, I promise. Let us prove it to you, however you want."

"Ah, the young friend of leopards speaks," Tangaroa said. The orangutan scampered around to put the old man between herself and Uraza. She squinted at the leopard from behind his back.

"Well, that's one thing," Conor interjected. "The Four Fallen came to us—surely that means we're on the side of the good Great Beasts, right?"

"Maaaaaaaaaaaybe," said Tangaroa. "Ngaio and I are not entirely convinced that leopards *can* be good, however. All of the ones we've met tend to look down their noses at us, as if they think the only thing orangutans are good for is eating."

Another growl rumbled in Uraza's throat, as if she was inclined to agree with that last statement. Abeke hurriedly stepped forward.

"Uraza would never eat Ngaio," she said. "And we aren't, uh, looking down at you. Not at all. Orangutans are—" *Oh, ack.* She didn't know anything about orangutans. "Uh, really . . . really great."

Tangaroa suddenly clapped his hands together. A flock of tiny yellow parrots bolted from a nearby tree into the sky. "I know! I know what would be fun! Great fun!"

Abeke could tell that Meilin was ready to stab something. *Fun* was not something any of them had time for, not with the future of Erdas at stake.

"What is it?" Abeke asked, keeping her voice as calm as she could.

"A test!" said the old man. "A chance to show off your skills and your bond with your spirit animal. If leopard girl can defeat my orangutan in a race, I'll tell you how to find Mulop."

Abeke looked at the furry orange ape. With Uraza's help, she could outrun an orangutan, couldn't she? And then perhaps she could prove to the others that she wasn't the mole—that she really was on their side.

"If that's what it takes," she said. "I'll do it."

"You shouldn't have to," Kalani said. "Grandfather, this is asking too much."

"Nothing is too much to ask for the honor of seeing Mulop," he retorted. "Leopard girl, there is a tree about a half mile that way, which was hit by lightning three days ago. Race Ngaio there and back, and whoever returns first—whoever touches this great boulder here first—shall be the winner."

"Wait," Tarik said, stepping forward. "I am their protector. Let me run in her place."

"No," said Tangaroa. "It must be the leopard girl." Ngaio slapped her hands together, grinning.

"I can do this," Abeke said to Tarik. "Really, I can."

He looked down at her with a serious expression. "I believe that," he said. "It's just a heavy burden to place on you, and if I can lighten it in any way . . . I wish I could, that's all."

"It's all right," she said, feeling the warmth of his caring like a small sun. Tarik protected them because it was his task, assigned by Olvan, but he also clearly worried about them and liked them too, and that was an even better sort of protection. Abeke couldn't help thinking that it would have been nice if her father had ever shown that kind of concern for her, instead of always worrying that she would shame their family.

"I can hold your cloak for you," Tarik offered, adding wryly, "Seems like the least I can do."

Abeke unhooked her cloak and handed him her bow and quiver as well.

"Good luck," he said, and behind him she saw Conor nodding too.

She knelt down so she could be face-to-face with Uraza. "Help me," she murmured to the leopard. Instantly a flood of power surged through her. She felt stronger, faster, and more attuned to the jungle. She could hear insects burrowing and branches creaking as parrots hopped through the treetops. She could smell the burned tree that was the marker for the race.

She stood up again. "Let's go."

They lined up beside each other. Ngaio stretched out her long arms and cracked her knuckles, then shook them out, flashing Abeke another grin.

Tangaroa bounced on the balls of his feet, clapping happily. "Racers ready?" he cried. "Be swift! Be sure! Be orangutans! GO!"

Abeke launched herself into a full-out sprint, leaping over creeping vines and mossy boulders as she tore through the jungle. For a moment she couldn't see Ngaio on either side of her, but her relief was cut short when she spotted the orangutan swinging rapidly through the trees up above. The spirit animal was already in the lead.

Cursing softly, Abeke tried to push her legs harder. It already felt as if the wind was lifting her, as if she flowed through the jungle swifter than a shadow. How could the orangutan be faster than her?

She called to Uraza with her mind and put on another burst of speed. She didn't dare look up again—her eyes were focused on the treacherous terrain ahead—but she thought she might have passed Ngaio, at least for now.

A rushing sound caught her attention from up ahead. Abeke smelled water and frogs, and before she'd cleared the trees, she knew.

A torrential river swept through the forest, right in her path.

Abeke skidded to a stop, looking frantically along the banks for a way across. *Not fair!* she thought. *Tangaroa knew this would slow me down.*

But not Ngaio. The orangutan flew by overhead, swinging effortlessly from vine to vine in the trees that reached over the river. Abeke could hear her laughter echoing through the leaves. In fact, Abeke was pretty sure there was a whole audience of monkeys up there laughing at her.

If she can get across that way, I can too.

Abeke bolted toward the nearest tree and scrambled up the trunk. It wasn't as easy as climbing a tree with the Granite Ram had been, but soon she was balancing on a branch high in the air, surveying the vines ahead of her. She needed to do this the smart way. She *had* to win this race—they needed that information.

Also, she was pretty sure she'd spotted at least one crocodile in the river down there. So her plan was to not fall in. Definitely no falling into the crocodile-infested river.

Abeke grabbed a vine, backed up, ran along the branch, and leaped into the air. The river rushed by below her boots, furiously pounding the rocks. At the end of her swing, she let go and grabbed for the next vine. For a terrifying moment, her hands fumbled with empty space, and then she felt them connect around the vine and her momentum hurled her forward again.

One more vine, one more heart-stopping unsupported leap through space—and then Abeke was swinging over land again. She was too high to let go and fall, though, so she flung herself at the closest branch. Her torso slammed into it, nearly knocking the breath out of her, and she clutched at the bark with her hands. She could feel herself slipping—sliding—and then her fingers caught on a knot in the wood and she hung there, her feet dangling over a fifteen-foot drop.

With a heave, Abeke kicked herself up until she was straddling the branch. She didn't have time to catch her breath. Ngaio was already much too far ahead. She might even be on her way back already.

I have to do that again on the return trip, Abeke realized, her heart dropping. She glanced out at the river and decided to worry about that when she had to.

Gathering her feet under her, she reached for the trunk of the tree.

And that's when she heard the noise.

It sounded like . . . it sounded like a little child crying.

Abeke scanned the jungle floor. *Where is it coming from?* She shook her head. She really, *really* didn't have time to stop and look for it.

But it sounded so sad, a kind of wordless, hiccupping cry of loneliness. The little yowls were relatively quiet, not a full-throated wail, as if the weeper had given up on anyone coming to help but still couldn't hold back the grief.

Wait. Abeke turned her head, tapping into her spirit animal senses to enhance her hearing.

The sound is coming from somewhere up here – somewhere in this tree, I think.

She knew the race was more important than anything. But she *couldn't* turn away from something that needed help.

She clambered around the trunk and spotted a kind of nest on a branch a short way over her head. As she climbed up to it, Abeke could see how large it was, made of branches and moss.

And sitting inside the nest, all alone, was a sobbing baby orangutan.

Little tufts of orange fur stuck up all over its head, and its tiny, humanlike feet were pressed together. The orangutan's face was buried in small dark hands. Its shoulders shook as it cried.

"Oh!" Abeke cried, her heart flooding with pity. At her gasp, the baby looked up and its huge, mournful brown eyes met hers. The race flew out of her head and she opened her arms toward it.

The baby stumbled over to her and wrapped its long arms around her neck, burying its face in her shoulder with a whimper. Its golden orange fur was soft and warm as it rested its whole weight trustingly against her, as if it would never let go. It reminded Abeke a little of Kunaya, the kitten she'd rescued on their trip to find Rumfuss.

She hugged it and whispered soothing nothings.

Now what do I do?

She couldn't possibly win the race with a baby orangutan clinging to her. But she couldn't abandon it here either. Tapping into her heightened senses from her bond with Uraza, she could both see and smell that no other orangutan had been here in days. Whatever had happened to its mother, this baby was all alone.

"Poor little guy," she murmured, stroking the baby's back. "It's all right. You're safe with me." She cuddled it closer and it squeaked pathetically.

Abeke heard rustling in the leaves and looked up.

Ngaio was in the next tree, staring down at Abeke and the baby orangutan.

7

THE CONCHES

CONOR SLAPPED THE SIDE OF HIS NECK.

"Too late," Rollan said. Conor felt the welt of the insect bite already rising under his fingers. He rubbed it, feeling itchy all over. The air buzzed, and tiny wings seemed to flicker across his skin whenever he stood still, but it was also too hot to keep moving.

Rollan swatted at one of the buzzing insects. "Tarik, please tell me they don't have the Sunset Death here." Conor touched the mosquito bite again with a shudder. He remembered all too clearly how ill Rollan had been in Zhong.

"I've seen it once or twice," Kalani answered before Tarik could. "It's rare, but we have banana gourd seeds in my village to cure it if we need to."

"That's good to know," Rollan said, "although I'd really prefer not to revisit the brink of death at all, if possible." He waved his arms even more vigorously and Meilin gave him a sharp stop-fooling-around glare.

"Shouldn't they be back by now?" she demanded.

Meilin hadn't stopped pacing around the clearing since the moment Abeke had raced off. Neither had Uraza. If he hadn't been so worried, Conor would have thought it was sort of funny, how similar they looked.

Tangaroa shrugged pacifically from the top of the boulder that marked the end of the race, where he was perched with his legs folded under him. Conor wished he could even pretend to be that calm. His skin prickled and sweat kept dripping into his eyes. Briggan came back from sniffing the undergrowth, licked Conor's hand, and sat down on his foot.

"You think she can do it, don't you?" Conor whispered to him.

Briggan gave him a thoughtful blue-eyed stare, which was not terribly reassuring.

Across the clearing, Uraza's head snapped up. She stared off into the trees where Abeke had disappeared. Her tail flicked menacingly. Tarik stepped over to stand beside her, snapping a small stick between his hands in an absentminded, worried way as he squinted at the jungle.

"They're coming," Tangaroa said. He unfolded himself from the rock and gazed up into the trees with a puzzled expression. "They're *both* coming. Ngaio?" he called.

But instead of swinging out of the trees, Ngaio emerged on the ground, walking side by side with Abeke. Curled in Abeke's arms was a small bundle of orange fur with a sweet, curious face. It sat up and peered at the gathering of people and animals in the clearing, and Conor realized it was a baby orangutan.

They reached the edge of the clearing and Ngaio stopped. She looked up at Abeke and indicated the boulder with one of her large, dark, humanlike hands.

"Ngaio, what are you doing?" Tangaroa asked. "Are you letting the leopard girl win?"

Abeke crossed to the boulder and put one hand on it, keeping the other one around the baby orangutan. She turned to Tangaroa. "My name is Abeke, not leopard girl," she said. "Now tell us how to find Mulop."

Tangaroa tugged on his lower lip. Ngaio ambled over to him and gently thwacked his arm, then waved at the baby Abeke was holding.

"I see," said the old man. "Very well, if that's what Ngaio wants."

"Yes!" Rollan yelped, throwing his fists in the air.

"Nice work, Abeke," Conor said. He felt like leaping around the clearing, but he didn't want to let on how worried he'd been.

"I knew you could do it," Tarik said, handing her cloak back to her with a grin.

"Kind of a weird way to win," Meilin huffed. Rollan and Conor both gave her a look, and she rolled her eyes. "I mean, yay, that's great."

Kalani crossed to Abeke and stroked the baby orangutan's head. "Cute," she said. "Almost as cute as a sea horse." The baby grabbed her hand and inspected each finger, then hopped down to the ground and started circling each stranger in turn.

"I was thinking we could call him Leopard," Abeke said, raising her eyebrows at Tangaroa.

"Ho ho! Ha ha ha!" Tangaroa threw his head back and bellowed with laughter. "I like it!"

Conor crouched to get level with Leopard, and the baby delightedly patted his face, squashed his nose, tugged on his hair, and finished by giving him a hug.

"Awwww," Conor said, chuckling.

"You big softie," Rollan observed, but he clearly couldn't help grinning at the little ape himself. Lumeo crept down from Tarik's shoulder and sniffed at the baby. The otter and the orangutan circled each other for a moment, and then suddenly Leopard leaped forward, Lumeo took off, and they began chasing each other playfully around the clearing.

"Ahem," Meilin said, putting her hands on her hips. She turned to Tangaroa. "You said something about a Kingray."

"Yes," he replied. "The Kingray can take you to Mulop—that's the only way to get there. You have to summon him by blowing two sacred conches together on Dagger Point."

Briggan yelped suddenly and whirled around to find the baby orangutan hanging from his tail. He spun in a circle and shook himself until Leopard tumbled off, then paced over to sniff at the baby.

Leopard seized his ears and promptly climbed on his head.

The wolf gave Conor a why-am-I-putting-up-with-this? look.

"Oh, you love it," Conor teased. Briggan was trying very hard to look dignified, but it would be hard for anyone, even a Great Beast, to maintain his dignity while wearing a bouncing orange hat.

"And where do we get these sacred conches?" Abeke asked Tangaroa.

"That is the tricky part," he admitted. "The white conch is hidden on Nightshade Island."

Kalani gasped and her hand flew to her mouth. "Grandfather! I can't believe you just said that!" she said in a low voice, glancing around as if the trees themselves might be listening.

"What? What's wrong with Nightshade Island?" Tarik asked.

"Let me guess," Rollan said. "Something evil."

"You can't go there," she said. "No one can. It's *tapu* — sacred, dangerous, and forbidden. We can't even speak of it." She shook her head again, her long braid flying behind her. "I . . . cannot help you."

"But if we went there without your help — ?" Conor guessed. "Maybe that would be okay?"

"Don't tell me about it," she insisted. "Don't even speak of it anymore. Grandfather, where is the black conch?"

"It's on Sunlight Island," Tangaroa said to Kalani. She winced.

"Sunlight Island! That doesn't sound so bad," Rollan said. "Oooh, I volunteer to go there."

"You're right, it wasn't bad at all — before the Conquerors came and made their base there," Kalani said. She touched her dolphin tattoo, her eyes downcast. "Now it's overrun with Conquerors, all of whom seem to have spirit animals somehow, and most of the animals there are creepy and monstrous. To give you an idea, my people have started calling it Monster Island."

"Fantastic," Rollan muttered. "I hereby unvolunteer."

"The Conquerors are using the Bile to force new spirit animal bonds," Tarik told Kalani. "That's why so many of them have companions — but they're not really companions, as the Bile bond turns the animals into slaves instead. They've also discovered that feeding the Bile to animals will make them larger, angrier, and more dangerous."

"By all the oceans," Kalani said with alarm. She touched the dolphin tattoo on her arm. "Forcing the spirit bond — that's horrible. And it explains a lot. I couldn't understand where so many Marked would have come from, or why they were all willing to help the Devourer attack my people." She frowned. "I wonder . . . one of my brothers didn't have a spirit animal . . . but I doubt he'd accept a bond that was unnatural."

Conor thought she didn't sound all that sure.

From his new perch on Briggan's head, the baby orangutan scanned them all and spotted Jhi for the first time. The giant panda was sitting in a patch of dappled sunlight with her front paws between her back paws, looking sleepy.

"Qrrrrr?" Leopard chirped at Ngaio, pointing at Jhi.

Ngaio spread her arms, as though she was saying, "I have no idea what that is either."

Leopard took a flying leap off Briggan's head and galloped over to Jhi. Before the panda could do more than blink in surprise, the little orangutan was clambering up her fur and inspecting her face with enthusiastic curiosity. Leopard poked the dark patches around Jhi's silver eyes a few times, then opened the panda's mouth and peeked inside.

Jhi let out an amused grunt and scooped the baby up in her paws. With Leopard hollering indignantly, Jhi set him on her shoulder and stood up to her full height.

"Oooooooorp," said the baby orangutan, clapping gleefully. He pointed down at everyone and chattered something imperious.

"I say we split up," Meilin said, ignoring Leopard's antics. "Two of us go to this Sunlight Island to find the black conch, while the other two—" She glanced at Kalani, who shook her head and pressed her fingers to her mouth. "While the other two do . . . something else. Something that doesn't involve Kalani."

"I can take you to Sunlight Island, but you'll need stealth to get past the Conquerors," Kalani pointed out.

"Then I say Abeke should do it," said Conor. "With Uraza's power, she should be perfect for that." Abeke smiled gratefully at him. "I'll go with her," he added. "If that's all right."

"Sure," Rollan said. "Meilin and I can go get the white OW!" he shouted as Meilin kicked him in the shin. He hopped away, scowling at her. "What was that for?"

Meilin jerked her head at Kalani, who had her hands over her ears. "She can't even hear about it, remember?" she whispered.

Rollan stomped off into the trees, muttering grumpily.

"You're right," Tarik said to Meilin, "but let's try a less physical way of making your point next time, if it's not too much trouble." He turned and bowed slightly to Kalani and Tangaroa. "Thank you for your help," he said. "Kalani, if you're willing to go with Abeke and Conor, I'll accompany Rollan and Meilin." She nodded.

"And then we'll meet you at Dagger Point once you have the conch," Meilin said to Conor. "Jhi, for the love of Mulop, would you stop rolling around like a drunk chimpanzee? Let's go."

The giant panda, who had been wrestling playfully with the baby orangutan, paused with a guilty expression and set the baby down. Leopard lifted up his arms and shrieked, demanding more play. Jhi shook her head, patted him gently, and followed Meilin and Tarik along Rollan's path into the jungle.

Leopard scampered back across the clearing and climbed into Abeke's arms again.

"I'm sorry, little guy," she said, giving him a hug. "I have to go too. But Ngaio will take good care of you — right?"

Ngaio nodded and reached out so the baby could clamber onto her back. Tangaroa smiled and wagged his head.

"I wish you luck, leopard girl," he said. "And you, wolf boy. Remember, Mulop is great and inscrutable, so be respectful and listen carefully. Also, wear something warm. It'll be a wetter sea voyage there than you're used to."

Conor felt like he could see for the first time why Tangaroa was called a "wise man." As if sensing Conor's thought, Tangaroa grinned impishly and jumped up to swing himself into the tree branches.

"Your turn to hide, Ngaio!" the old man called, and in a moment, the orangutans and Tangaroa had all vanished into the leaves.

8

NIGHTSHADE ISLAND

NIGHT HAD FALLEN. GLITTERING STARS STRETCHED ACROSS the dark southern sky in constellations that Meilin had studied in books, but had never seen before. She wished her father were here to see them too. He'd traveled all across Zhong, but she didn't think he'd ever been to Oceanus.

And now he never will.

Meilin wrapped her hand around the hilt of the sword in her belt, taking comfort from the weight of the weapon. She pushed aside the memories of her father and focused on the moonlit beach before them, lined with canoes that had been pulled up onto the sand. The smoky smell of fires rose from the village in the distance, and orange torches flickered as the islanders prepared for sleep.

"I still don't get it," Rollan hissed. "The people here like us. They saved us from the bad guys, right? They did stuff to heal the whales. So why can't we just *ask* them for a canoe?"

"Since when did *you* develop a problem with stealing?" Meilin asked him.

"I have my honor," Rollan said haughtily. "I only steal—I mean, stole—from people who deserved it."

"Meaning people who had stuff you wanted?" Meilin guessed.

"No," Rollan said sharply, surprising Meilin with his seriousness. "Meaning people who'd rather throw a meal away than give it to a starving orphan." He sighed and waved his hands at the murmuring village. "But they would help us. I bet you anything they'd be all, 'Hey, sure, of course, take six canoes if you like, and here's some strong cheerful friends to help paddle them for you too.'"

"Aha," Meilin said. "The truth comes out. You just don't want to row one of those things all by ourselves."

"I am *trying* to do the *ethically responsible* thing here," he insisted.

"That's what we are doing," Tarik cut in. He'd been studying the canoes as well, turning a small whittling knife between his hands. His dark green cloak blended into the shadows. Lumeo was coiled around his shoulders, breathing gently as if asleep.

Meilin was sure she and Rollan could get the conch by themselves . . . but she was still relieved that Tarik had decided to come along.

"Wait, what?" Rollan asked Tarik. "Stealing a canoe is the right thing to do?"

"We are protecting the islanders," Tarik said to him. "*Tapu* is a very powerful thing. If anyone knew where we were going—if anyone spoke of this island to us—if someone helped us get there even just by giving us a canoe—then they would be marked as *tapu* as well. They could be exiled; at the very least, they would have to be cleansed."

"Sounds like you're not talking about a bath," Rollan observed.

"The cleansing ceremony is sacred and secret," Tarik said. "I don't know anything about it. But we are not subjecting any of these good people to the guilt and anxiety and social ostracism that comes when you associate yourself with anything *tapu*. Better to steal a canoe and go without anyone knowing about it."

"And besides, we'll bring it back tomorrow," Meilin said.

Tarik shook his head, a stirring of shadows in the bushes. "We can't. Once it touches that island, the canoe will be *tapu* as well. We'll have to destroy it for them, and pay for it some other way."

"Huh," Rollan said. "Doesn't that mean *we'll* be *tapu* as well, if we go there? So if we're trying to follow their rules as much as possible, then no one should talk to us either?"

Tarik thought about that for a long moment. "You're right," he admitted.

"Whoa," Meilin said to Rollan. "Bet you've never heard *that* before. Are you okay? I'm sure this comes as a bit of a shock."

"Ha ha ha," Rollan retorted brilliantly.

"I'll think about that," Tarik said. "Thank you, Rollan, it's a good point."

Rollan subsided, looking entirely too pleased with himself.

"Oh, dear," Meilin said. "I'm not sure his head is going to fit in the canoe anymore."

Rollan snorted with amusement, but Tarik was quiet, looking toward the lights of the village. After a moment, he sighed heavily. "This quest is leaving a lot of burned bridges in our wake. I fear we, and perhaps all Greencloaks by extension, will no longer be so welcome afterward in places like this."

"And the Ice City, and Samis," Meilin said, guessing where his thoughts had gone. By waking Suka the Polar Bear in Arctica, they had destroyed the Ardu's frozen city. And she guessed that Suka's pond in Samis no longer gave everlasting life to anyone who drank from it. That was sure to have earned them a great deal of enmity.

"We do what we must," Tarik said. "As long as we save Erdas — and as long as you all are safe — that's what's important." He clapped Rollan on the back. "It's quiet enough now. Let's take that one."

Tarik pointed at the smallest canoe, then darted out across the beach toward it. Meilin and Rollan followed, their boots slipping and sinking into the soft sand.

Tarik knelt and sliced through the rope that tied the canoe to the others on the beach. Meilin took the end closest to the water and heaved it toward the ocean. She was surprised at how light it was.

Waves rushed up over her feet with a hurrying, swishing sound, like hundreds of warriors marching far away. The water tugged at her legs as it whooshed back, and she had to catch her balance before she climbed into the canoe.

The boat rocked lightly as Tarik jumped in at the back,

and then again, violently, nearly tipping over as Rollan dragged himself onboard as well. Tarik reached forward and caught Rollan's arm, helping him up.

And then they were away, paddling as quietly as they could through the starry night. Meilin glanced down at the dark ocean and tried not to think of slavering shark jaws coming right at her.

"Do we know where we're going?" Rollan asked once the island was out of sight. "Because I'm guessing we can't ask anyone for directions."

"Nightshade Island was erased from the maps of Erdas after the last war," Tarik said.

"So . . . no," Rollan answered himself.

"Which means we need a little help," Tarik said. "Perhaps from someone with extremely sharp eyesight who can fly?" Meilin felt the canoe rock as he poked Rollan with his foot.

"Oh, you mean my very agreeable spirit animal," Rollan said. "Right, that's definitely going to work." But he held up his arm and looked at the sky hopefully.

Meilin touched the panda tattoo on her own arm, wishing Jhi could do something to help.

With a flutter of wings, Essix descended and settled on the side of the canoe. In the bright moonlight, her feathers looked silver and black. Her sharp talons curled around the wood and she tilted her head at Rollan.

"We need your help," Rollan said. "We're, uh—we're looking for an island."

Essix shifted her gaze to Tarik. If she'd had eyebrows, Meilin guessed her expression would have been priceless.

"I know, I know," Rollan said. "There's a hundred to choose from, ha ha ha. But we're looking for a specific one – Nightshade Island."

The falcon let out a shriek that nearly blasted out Meilin's eardrums. The bird's feathers all ruffled up around her neck, she glared at Rollan as if he'd suggested something even worse than a return trip to Arctica.

"Ow," Rollan protested, rubbing his ears. "What's the matter with you? You know this place?"

Essix shrieked again and shuffled over to jab at Rollan's knee with her wickedly hooked beak.

"OW!" Rollan yelled. "Tarik, a little help? Why is she so mad?"

"Rumor has it that something dark happened on Nightshade Island during the last war," Tarik said thoughtfully. "Maybe Essix knows what it was. Maybe she was there. Or maybe she only knows it's a bad place." He stopped paddling and reached up to pat Lumeo. "I hope we're not making a grave mistake, going there."

Essix let out another bloodcurdling shriek.

"Yes, all right, we know what *you* think," Rollan grumbled. "Can you lead us there anyway?" He paused, then added, "Please?"

"Essix, it's the only way we'll get to see Mulop," Meilin chimed in. "We need his talisman if we're going to stop the Devourer. So we have to go to Nightshade Island to find the white conch, no matter how dangerous it is."

The falcon clacked her beak several times as if annoyed. Abruptly she lifted into the air and soared ahead of them, veering northeast.

"Hmm. I don't know if that's a 'yes' or a 'go eat worms,'" Rollan admitted.

"So we follow her," Meilin said, "and we just have to hope she's taking us to the island, right?"

Tarik didn't answer, but he steered the canoe in the direction Essix had gone. They all paddled silently after the falcon.

———◆———

Meilin was usually excellent at keeping track of time. She could make herself wake up at sunrise; she could calculate in her head the minutes it would take to do any task. Even with all the traveling they'd been doing lately, she was still usually quite certain when it was time for the night to be over and the sun to be up.

And right now the answer was: at least two hours ago.

She set the paddle carefully across the canoe in front of her and rubbed her eyes. Why was it still so dark? Yes, she could tell they were surrounded by a thick fog, but even so, it should have gotten a little bit lighter once it was morning. But the water was blacker than ever, the moon and stars blotted out by the rolling murkiness around them. When she twisted around, she could barely see Rollan, sitting in the middle of the canoe only a few feet behind her. Beyond him, Tarik was a lump of darkness.

Meilin wished there was space in the canoe to release Jhi. She could really use some heightened senses right about now.

Up ahead, they heard the screeching call of the falcon

again. They hadn't seen her in hours; they were just trying to follow the sound of her voice.

Tarik adjusted the direction of the canoe and spoke quietly. "I know, Meilin. Something's wrong. Lumeo can feel it too."

"Maybe we should go back," Rollan suggested.

"I'm not sure we can," Tarik said. "I suspect we've been paddling in circles for a while; I have no idea which way is out or back. I'm not even sure we're really hearing Essix anymore. My guess is that this island really doesn't want to be found."

A dozen paper-thin spiders seemed to be scuttling down Meilin's spine; she shivered and felt for her sword hilt again. What kind of place could magically repel visitors? Where did this fog come from?

"On the plus side," she said, "that probably means we're close. Right?"

"Essix!" Rollan suddenly shouted, cupping his hands around his mouth. "ESSIX! Come back!" His voice faded into the clouds that surrounded them, absorbed like ink marks on wet paper.

There was no response, no answering screech or flurry of wingbeats. They waited in silence for a long moment.

"Where is she?" Rollan asked. "ESSIX! What do you mean, we weren't really hearing her? What have we been hearing — and what happened to Essix? And why didn't you say anything sooner?"

"I wasn't sure," Tarik said. "I'm still not sure. But I think the fog is playing tricks on us."

Meilin leaned back and put a reassuring hand on

Rollan's knee. "I'm sure Essix is all right. Probably better off than we are. She's smart and resourceful and tough, remember? I bet she's in the sunshine somewhere, eating a lizard and thinking we're all idiots for not having found her yet."

Rollan didn't say anything, but after a moment, she felt his fingers twine around hers. It was comforting, how large and warm his hands were. Like leaning into a furry, solid panda.

They sat like that for a minute, holding hands while the boat drifted. Tarik had stopped paddling as well and seemed to be listening.

"Do either of you hear that?" he whispered.

"What?" Rollan whispered back; Meilin just tilted her head and concentrated.

A soft whooshing sound echoed somewhere nearby . . . in and out, in and out . . . like armies on the move.

"Waves breaking on shore," said Meilin. She listened for a moment longer, then pointed. "That way."

Tarik wordlessly turned the canoe, and they paddled with new energy.

Meilin still couldn't see anything but billowing fog when she heard sand crunching under the bottom of the boat. She leaned over and jabbed her paddle into what turned out to be solid land.

"We've hit a beach, I think," she said. Cautiously she stepped out of the canoe and edged forward. The sand under her sloped up out of the water. For a moment, the fog cleared just a little, and she saw a beach of black sand, studded with broken shells that looked like shards of bone.

Maybe that's what they are. Who knows what horrible thing happened here – maybe a terrible battle.

There was no doubt in her mind that this was Nightshade Island. The weight of something evil hunkered over the whole place. If the word *tapu* hadn't already existed, Meilin thought someone would have invented it just to describe this island. Dangerous and forbidden – a place no one should ever go, or touch, or even speak of.

We definitely shouldn't be here.

But we have no choice.

She grabbed the front of the canoe and dragged it up on the sand; Rollan and Tarik jumped out to help her. They carried it as far from the water as they could. None of them were sure if it was high tide or low tide at the moment, or what that meant on this island, but they didn't want to risk the possibility of waves coming in and carrying off their only way out of here.

As soon as the canoe was secure, with a few large rocks piled around it to anchor it into the sand, Meilin held out her arm and released Jhi.

The panda stood beside her for a long moment, staring around at the fog. Slowly she sat down and gave Meilin a troubled look. Her silver eyes gleamed and her giant paws left deep indentations in the black sand.

And yet, it almost seemed like she wasn't there at all. Meilin could *see* her, but the usual waves of serenity and strength that came with the panda's appearance were missing. Meilin hadn't quite realized how strong their connection was until she couldn't feel it, and now it was like one of her senses was missing.

"Jhi?" she said softly, holding out her hand.

The panda pressed her nose into Meilin's fingers, but even that didn't help. It still seemed like a ghost was standing in front of her, even though it was a ghost with fur that she could touch.

"Is everything all right?" Rollan asked.

Meilin shook her head. She could tell that Jhi didn't want to be here either, the same way Essix had resisted. She had a feeling Jhi knew exactly what terrible thing had happened here. But the panda would still help her; it was muffled, but Meilin could still feel something, a kind of sense of direction. The vortex of the evil or the magic or the disruption, whatever had happened here, seemed to be at the center of the island. She let go of Jhi and strode ahead of the others, heading for the interior of the island.

As they moved farther inland, the black sand turned into a pebbly stretch of jagged black rocks. The sharp edges dug into the bottom of Meilin's boots. It was hard to travel in a straight line, with ankle-turning crevices lurking everywhere underfoot.

After a minute, she felt Rollan's hand brush against hers and their fingers intertwined again. In the misty gloom, he felt like an anchor to the real world, even more real than Jhi. Like all the rest of her might drift away, but her hand would still be there, safely wrapped in his.

It was a little weird if she thought about it, and a little weird that she liked it, and a little weird to think about Rollan at all when she needed to focus on finding the white conch and getting out of here. She wished she could think of something sharp and teasing to say that would make everything feel normal again. But none of them seemed to feel like talking; it was as though the air was too heavy for speech.

A huge, gnarled shape loomed suddenly in front of them, and Meilin jumped back, her free hand grabbing for her sword.

"It's a tree," Rollan whispered. He paused, then made the effort to add, "But I bet you can still defeat it. Just glare at it for a minute. Yeah, like that." He managed a grin, and she felt herself smiling back.

"It's already dead," Tarik said, walking around the tree. He touched it lightly with one hand. "It feels petrified. Like stone. What could have done this?"

Meilin ran her fingers along the smooth, cold bark. Tarik was right. It felt like a statue. A statue of a tree that had been blasted by lightning, or something worse.

"Whoa," Rollan said under his breath, squeezing Meilin's hand. She turned and saw more shapes through the fog – more petrified trees, all of them twisted and knotted, pale and bent.

Something moved on one of the branches.

Meilin had her knife out in a heartbeat, ready to throw, and realized in the nick of time that the something was Essix.

"Essix!" Rollan yelled, letting go of Meilin and running forward.

The falcon turned her head slowly and looked at him with vast disinterest.

"You're all right." Rollan leaned against the tree where Essix was perched. "I couldn't feel you at all." The falcon didn't move. "Essix?" He turned to Tarik. "I still can't— I mean, it's like she's barely there at all. Barely *here*." He touched his chest.

"It's the island," Meilin said. "Even Jhi—it's like she's behind glass." She found Jhi beside her and ran her hand over the panda's soft black ears.

"This place is affecting our spirit animal bonds," Tarik said, sounding wretched. He held Lumeo gently in his hands, but the otter was gazing almost blankly out at the fog. Meilin had never seen the little animal so passive and limp before.

"Essix?" Rollan said, shoving his hands in his pockets and hunching his shoulders. "Are you all right?"

"I'm going to put Lumeo into dormant state while we're here," Tarik said. "I think it'll be safer for him . . . for us. I recommend you both do the same." The otter curled toward Tarik and then vanished.

Meilin shook her head. "It's all right. I can still control Jhi. And I need the extra alertness, or else I might fall asleep on my feet." She noticed that Tarik and Rollan were frowning. "What?"

"You shouldn't think of it as controlling her," Tarik said.

"Yeah," Rollan agreed. "Your spirit animal is more like a partner, right, Tarik?"

"Says the last one of us to get his animal into dormant state," Meilin snapped. "Why would I take any advice from you? Jhi and I have a much better relationship than you and Essix." She put one arm over the panda's furry back.

"Hey," Rollan said. "That's just mean."

Meilin knew, with a pang of regret, that she had been

hurtful. But she didn't need anyone telling her how to interact with her own spirit animal. Jhi was fine.

"Let's all calm down," Tarik interjected. "The island is going to affect us all badly. We should find the conch so we can get out of here as soon as possible."

Rollan looked up at Essix. Hesitantly, he opened his shirt and waited. Meilin could tell that he wasn't at all sure the falcon would go into passive state. She didn't seem inclined to acknowledge him at all.

Essix stared up at the sky for a long moment. Finally she clacked her beak twice, spread her wings, and vanished into the tattoo on Rollan's chest.

Rollan exhaled with relief.

"I think it's this way somewhere," Meilin said, walking past the trees. "It feels — darker in this direction." She glanced back at the others, who nodded and followed her.

What had happened here? What could be so bad that it left echoes of evil lingering so long after the last great war?

More trees twisted out of the fog all around them as they walked. They trekked for a long time, through a landscape that didn't seem to change very much. It was a bit like their endless night of paddling. Meilin's eyes were heavy and her feet dragged. She wished she could sleep, but she couldn't imagine letting her guard down enough to do that in a place like this.

The fog wound creepily around her legs, gray now instead of completely black. Maybe there was still a sun out there after all, far beyond this horrible place. Meilin could only see a few paces in front of her.

She realized she couldn't hear or sense Jhi behind her.

But she knew the panda had to be there. She had to be. She was always there.

Meilin stopped and looked back. Nothing: She couldn't see Tarik or Rollan either. But they must be right behind her. If she just waited for a moment, they would step into sight. And then Jhi would come ambling up behind them.

It wasn't possible to lose your spirit animal. Not even in a place like this. Right?

Maybe she should have listened to Tarik.

She remembered Lord MacDonnell's hare, who'd left him after the lord treated him poorly. And Finn's wildcat, who had entered passive state and refused to come out for a long time.

What would she do if Jhi *didn't* wander out of the fog?

Tarik and Rollan appeared, walking side by side. They leaned toward each other a little, looking almost like father and son with their matching dark hair and tan skin. Meilin felt a twist of sadness again. Why did everything have to remind her of her father?

They saw her waiting and stopped too.

"Looking for Jhi?" Tarik asked softly.

Meilin nodded. She didn't trust herself to speak.

Silence fell. Nothing emerged from the fog. There were no sounds of footfalls on the rocks, no flash of black-and-white fur through the mist.

No Jhi.

Meilin pulled her cloak closer, shivering in the damp, eerie air.

The panda would come. She *had* to come.

More long moments passed. Rollan sidled up beside her, and when she didn't protest, he put one arm around her.

"She'll be here in a minute," he whispered.

Meilin nodded again.

And waited.

9

SUNLIGHT ISLAND

CONOR WOULD GIVE SUNLIGHT ISLAND ONE THING: IT WAS definitely sunny.

Too sunny. Bright and cheerful and glorious. Palm trees swayed against an azure blue sky; the brilliant white seagulls overhead were nearly as dazzling as mirrors in the blazing light.

It seemed like entirely the wrong place for the forces of the Devourer to be gathered, and yet, there they were—long ships anchored in the bay, men and women swarming between the beach and the jungle with boxes of supplies and weaponry. And, everywhere, animals: hideous, gargantuan, vicious-looking animals.

Snarling tigers paced beside sniggering hyenas on the sand. A wild-eyed baboon shrieked and gibbered at a pair of large-eared caracals, while a scaly anteater scraped at a tree nearby. Three vultures were perched on ship masts, eyeing the people below with what looked like grim patience. And there were more snakes and giant spiders and species of crocodile crawling around than Conor wanted to think about.

Moreover, all this sunshine made it nearly impossible to hide, or move, or do anything stealthy at all. Conor, Abeke, and Kalani had spent most of the day lying in a shallow hole, covered with palm fronds. They could peek out and see the center of the Conquerors' operations, but hopefully nobody would notice them. They were waiting for it to get dark.

Although even then, there could be eyes everywhere — owls, and bats, and other night predators working for the Devourer.

He hoped their canoe would be safe where they'd hidden it.

Conor wished he could release Briggan. He'd feel much better with his wolf lying alongside him. In the green light that filtered through the palm fronds, he'd noticed Abeke's fingers twitching as if she wanted to be running them through Uraza's fur. The only one who was completely calm was Kalani. She'd wrapped her feather cloak around her and fallen asleep close to midday. Strands of hair had fallen out of her long dark braid and spilled over the jade green swirls of tattoos on her arms and shoulders.

Maybe she's more accustomed to separation from her animal, since she's bonded to a sea creature. Conor thought about her dolphin, and how strange it would be to have to go into the water every time you needed to train or communicate with your spirit animal.

And how does it feel to become queen of your people so young, and in such a sad way? he wondered. He envied her air of confidence and leadership, but not her story.

"The sun's finally setting," Abeke murmured, stretching as well as she could in the cramped space.

"How are we going to look for the conch?" Conor whispered. "What if it's right in the Conquerors' camp or something?"

Kalani opened her eyes, and he wondered how long she'd been awake. "There's a system of caves that runs under the island," she whispered. "I think we should look there first. If I were hiding something on Sunlight Island, that's where I'd take it."

"That makes sense," Abeke agreed softly, and Conor nodded too.

As soon as darkness had spread its quiet wings over the island, the three of them lifted the palm fronds and crept out of their hiding spot. They could still hear voices and a cacophony of screeches and animal sounds down in the camp.

Abeke released Uraza immediately and Conor did the same, feeling his whole body relax as his fingers touched Briggan's fur. Instantly he could sense a million more details about the night. He could smell the burning palm fronds in the campfires and the cracked coconuts some of the men were sharing. He could hear hissing underneath the loud voices, and the splash of some large predator moving through the bay. He could feel a light breeze lifting the hair on his arms. And even as the night grew darker, it seemed like his eyesight sharpened.

That all made it easier to follow Abeke as she crept through the trees, although she moved so lightly, it was often impossible to see or hear either her or Uraza. Kalani pointed in the direction of the caves and Abeke led the way, pausing now and then to listen, or signaling them to wait while she scouted for lookouts and spies.

If she was the mole, I could be in a lot of trouble right now, Conor thought on one of these occasions, when Abeke had disappeared soundlessly into the brush. What if she came back with a platoon of warriors to trap him? He had the Slate Elephant tucked in his pocket, given to him by Tarik when he'd heard their plan.

On the one hand, it was nice to have the security of a talisman in case a fight broke out. On the other hand, it was a big responsibility. If they got caught, that would mean one more talisman in the Devourer's hands.

He shook himself, feeling guilty. *Abeke isn't going to betray me. She's not the mole. She wouldn't do that.*

But . . . who *would*?

"Coast is clear," Abeke's voice breathed from the shadows, and they crept forward again, edging down a slope. At the bottom Conor spotted a yawning hole in the side of the hill. If this was the entrance to the caves, it was a lot smaller than he'd hoped for. They'd have to crawl inside.

It was, and they did. They crawled several feet, in fact, before reaching a spot where they could stand, where Kalani lit a torch and Conor was able to study the caves around them. The damp rock walls pressed in close, giving Conor that same claustrophobic feeling he got inside castles like the Earl of Trunswick's. Here there was a lot less space and no soaring ceilings, but the sensation of being trapped inside, too far from freedom and air and light, was the same.

Now Kalani went first, marking the turns they took with a stick that glowed faintly in the dark and left luminescent trails on the stone walls. Conor wasn't sure what system she was using for the symbols. He felt instantly lost in the winding, labyrinthine tunnels, and it seemed like they kept circling back to the same marks, but Kalani walked on confidently with an unworried expression.

They searched methodically, exploring each branching tunnel and dead end. Sometimes they could walk upright; more often they had to crouch, and a few times they crawled on hands and knees through unpleasantly tight spots. Uraza and Briggan squeezed along behind them, both of them sniffing the air and pawing at dark corners.

It seemed like hours passed before they came across something new: a trickling stream flowing along one of the side tunnels and down into darkness. "How big is this cave system?" Conor asked as they stopped to refill their flasks.

Kalani shrugged, sending firelit shadows dancing and jumping behind her. "No one has ever mapped it. I don't know."

All at once, Uraza growled. Abeke scrambled to her feet and peered upstream. "What was that?" she whispered.

Conor and Kalani fell silent, and Conor's sharpened hearing caught the sound too: footsteps, coming this way.

There was no time to hide; the tunnel was straight enough that whoever it was would have already seen their torch. Conor drew his ax and reached for Briggan. At least it sounded like only one person. *One Conqueror.*

The approaching figure reached the edge of their circle of light, paused, and stepped forward so his face was visible: nut brown as Kalani's, with the same nose and wide eyes. He had closely shaved dark hair and tattoos like waves winding across his nose and cheeks.

"Timote!" Kalani cried. She thrust the torch at Conor and jumped forward to wrap her arms around the young man. He swayed slightly, blinking in an unfocused way, and then shook himself, pulled her away to arm's length, and squinted at her.

"Kalani?" he said. "What are you doing here?"

"We were looking for the black conch," she said. "But I didn't know you were here! I thought—I was afraid that—Where's Piri? Are you both all right?"

"Better than all right," he said, letting go of her and stepping back. "You shouldn't have come here."

"We can get you out," Kalani said. "These are my friends—we have a canoe—we can be gone before morning. We can take you home." She tried to clasp his hand again, and he moved out of reach. "Brother? What's wrong?"

"I'm not one of you anymore," he said in a hoarse, strained voice. "I know that you're the queen now. Do you expect me to come back and bow down to you? Or were you planning on handing the crown right over to me?"

Kalani stared at him, then drew herself up to her full regal height. "I'm not worried about that right now. What's important is to get you and Piri to safety."

"You can't take us anywhere near the tribe!" Timote exploded. He paused, flexing his tattooed fists. "And we wouldn't go, in any case. Do you remember my spirit animal, Kalani?" he asked.

"Waka?" she said uneasily. "Of course."

His face muscles twisted into a bitter smile. "Do you remember how he resisted me? How he refused to go into dormant mode? How he would stand there watching me with mocking eyes every time I asked him to do anything?"

Conor had an awful feeling he knew where this was going.

Timote turned and snapped his fingers at the tunnel behind him. There was a slow, painful scraping noise, and a few minutes later an emu hobbled up to stand beside Kalani's brother.

Abeke stiffened beside Conor, pressing her hands to her mouth. He just barely managed to hold back a gasp himself.

The bird was taller than either Kalani or Timote, but his long neck drooped and he shuffled in an awkward way. His shaggy brown feathers were patchy and ragged and his eyes were half-closed. One of his claws was jaggedly broken, which explained the limping and the scraping sound.

"Oh, no," Kalani whispered. "Timote, what have you done?"

"My animal does what I tell him to now," he said smugly. "I always knew he could be a strong, vicious weapon if he would stop fighting *me* and start fighting whomever I told him to. Now I can make him attack anyone I want." He glanced meaningfully at Conor.

"But he's hurt," Abeke said. Her hand lifted, as if she

couldn't stop herself from trying to help the wounded bird.

"That's why we're here," Timote said. "This stream is supposed to have healing properties. I'm not a monster, Kalani; stop looking at me like that. I fix him up again afterward. It's just such a relief to have Waka listen to me now. You can't understand; you and Katoa fit together like fish scales. But for me — imagine, no more pleading, no more bargaining or useless flattery — just, hey, emu, go kick that tiger, and it's done. And all thanks to this little drink the Reptile King gave me. Is it any wonder I'm happy to stay and fight by his side?"

Kalani shuddered. "What about Piri?" she said softly.

"He's happier too," said Timote, as sharply as if he were trying to drive a knife into her chest. "He's always wanted a spirit animal, and the Bile gave him one. In fact, he got to pick. He chose a killer whale — it's great. If I could start over and choose for myself, I'd pick one of those too."

The emu's head hung even lower, and Conor felt like his heart might break for the once-proud, once-independent bird.

"So that's it," Kalani said. "You both work for the enemy now, even though they killed Mother and Father."

Timote stood looking down at her for a moment. Kalani's brother swayed slightly, then caught himself and frowned at her.

"Mother and Father belonged to the old world," he said. "The Reptile King is going to change everything. He's giving the power of the spirit animal bond to everyone! He's uniting the continents and his army is —"

Kalani punched him in the face.

It was so powerful and so fast, Conor didn't quite realize what had happened until Timote keeled over backward and crashed to the floor.

"Oh!" Abeke yelped with surprise.

"That should shut him up for a while," Kalani said calmly, shaking her hand out. "That no-good shark-faced backstabbing son of a jellyfish." She turned to Waka, who was nudging Timote mournfully with his beak, and rested her hand lightly on the emu's back. "I'm so sorry, Waka. Would you—would you escape with us? I promise I'll look after you. You can hide in our village as long as you want."

The emu lifted his injured foot and warbled something, then slowly lowered himself to sit beside Timote. Even after everything Timote had done to him, he wouldn't leave him.

Conor rubbed his teary eyes. He couldn't imagine someone getting the gift of a spirit animal and then abusing it this way. He reached for the comfort of Briggan's fur and the wolf leaned into him, as if he needed comforting as well.

"We'd better get out of here as fast as we can," Abeke said. "If the Conquerors can get inside the heads of anyone who's drunk the Bile, they probably know we're here now."

Kalani nodded and gave her unconscious brother one last, heartbroken look. Then she turned to take the torch again, setting her chin in a determined, queenly way. "There are a lot of tunnels still to search," she warned them.

Briggan growled slightly, and Conor had a sudden thought.

"Briggan used to be called Pathfinder, back when he

was a Great Beast. Maybe he has some . . . vision skills that could at least narrow down the search."

He crouched so he was nose to nose with the wolf. "Any ideas? Please help us," he whispered. "We could really use it right now. A black conch – that's like a giant seashell. Is it even in these caves?"

Briggan sat back, grinning his wolfish grin, and put one paw over Conor's hand on the floor.

Conor closed his eyes and breathed deeply. He waited for an image to appear in his head. A long moment passed . . . and then something new caught his attention.

Not a vision . . . a smell.

It was faint, but different from the other damp underground earthy smells of the caves.

It smelled like the deep ocean, like giant ancient sea snails sliding quietly along the bottom of the sea.

He opened his eyes and looked into Briggan's deep blue gaze. The wolf tilted his head.

"Let's look down here," Conor said to the others, pointing to a narrow tunnel that sloped in the direction of the scent.

Kalani opened her mouth, perhaps to argue, but Abeke touched her shoulder lightly and nodded at Conor. He felt a twist of guilt for his earlier worries. She had faith in him. He ought to have the same faith in her.

They left the emu and Timote by the stream. Conor went first, trying to move faster despite slipping on the damp rocks. At the bottom, he breathed in until he figured out the smell was coming from his left, and then he led them in that direction.

More twists, more turns, more dark cave walls pressing in on them. Conor hoped Kalani was keeping track of where they were going, because he wasn't sure how they'd ever get back.

And then, all at once, the tunnel opened into a small, perfectly round cave. Up above them, moonlight drifted down through a circular hole in the ceiling, illuminating the space. Another tunnel led away from the cave, and at the end of it Conor could see more moonlight glowing – a path to the outside.

But more importantly: A shelf was carved in the back wall of the cave, and perched on that shelf, directly in the light of the moon, was a giant black conch shell.

Conor darted over to it with a gasp of triumph. Its edges rippled like frozen black water, and the points were wickedly sharp. He lifted it with caution. It weighed as much as one of the silver serving bowls in the Earl of Trunswick's castle.

"It's beautiful," Kalani whispered reverently.

"Let's get out of here," Abeke suggested.

They ran down the tunnel that led toward the moonlight. But as they felt the night wind on their faces, suddenly Briggan growled and Uraza stopped, crouching and flicking her tail.

"What is it?" Conor asked, his heart sinking.

A horrible hiss answered him from the cave entrance.

Kalani raised the torch and they all saw what their animals had sensed first.

Blocking their exit was a huge and deadly Komodo dragon.

10

THE SCREAMING
TREES

ROLLAN REMEMBERED STANDING IN THE FOG WITH HIS ARM around Meilin. He remembered being tired all the way through his toes. He remembered waiting in silence; he remembered staring helplessly into the dark, which was resolutely empty of giant pandas.

He did not remember how he'd gotten here, to the outskirts of a circle of white trees. The fog was gone; the sun shone thinly from behind pale morning clouds.

This couldn't be Nightshade Island. Plants were growing here, and small animals rustled in the undergrowth. Everything smelled clean and fresh.

Everything, that is, except for the horrifyingly enormous silverback gorilla, taller than the walls around Concorba, looming in the center of the clearing.

He smelled pretty awful.

The gorilla squinted in Rollan's direction, as if he'd heard that thought.

Rollan flinched. He might not have had tutors and years of studying, but he certainly knew who the only giant gorilla in the world was.

This had to be Kovo, the Great Ape, who had been aligned with the Devourer in the war.

He was quite definitely on the bad guy list.

But shouldn't he be in prison? Rollan wondered. *How and when did he get out? And where are Tarik and Meilin?*

If the gorilla saw Rollan, he ignored him. Instead Kovo turned back to the far side of the trees, where a boy stood, warily watching the gorilla.

The boy, who looked barely older than Rollan, wore a short travel cloak of fine, deep red velvet, and on his head was a crown. Despite his age, he held himself like a king — a nervous king, facing such a menacing Great Beast, but a king nonetheless. Opals set into the gold crown glinted in the sunshine. His eyes were hard and brown, and he had an arrogant way of holding his head. Something about him was vaguely familiar.

The boy king drew his cloak closer around him. "You . . . you propose we go to war with our neighbors?"

Rollan realized he'd arrived mid-conversation. *Oh. I'm dreaming.* This had to be a dream — but it felt awfully real.

"War is inevitable in your species, I'm afraid," said Kovo in a dark, rumbling voice that seemed to echo both inside and outside Rollan's head. "The question is whether your people will go to war with you — *for* you — or against you. Now, do not look so crestfallen. There is plenty of time to turn things around."

"My father spoke of war as a great evil."

"Your father lived in simpler times. That's not really fair either, if you think about it. He left all of Stetriol's problems to you. But I come to you now with solutions. Take the land you deserve. Arm your people with iron and steel . . . and this." Kovo held out his hand, revealing a small glass vial.

"Go on," he said. Rollan could feel the weight of the power behind those words. Who could say no to Kovo? Who would dare?

The king hesitated only a moment, then stepped forward and accepted the vial. He clutched it to his chest and took three steps quickly back. Then he stared down at the amber liquid inside, greed and ambition written across his face, but also hesitation.

No! Rollan wanted to scream. *It's a trick! Once you drink it, they'll control you!* He clenched his fists, thinking of his mother. If only someone had been there to stop her. *If only the Bile didn't exist in the first place.*

Kovo moved his mouth into something horribly like a smile, but not.

"The Bile . . . the bond it brings," said the boy. "It will make me stronger? Faster?"

"The gifts vary from bond to bond. But each bond does bring gifts. And you . . ." Kovo spread his massive, hairy arms. "You have the pick of the litter."

Animals burst out of the forest, crawling or flying or walking toward the pair in the clearing. It seemed to Rollan as though every creature he could think of was suddenly here, swarming around the king, waiting to be chosen.

The boy looked around, a crooked half smile forming

on his lips. He lifted the vial toward Kovo in a kind of salute, then drank the whole thing down.

All the trees began to scream.

At least, that's what it felt like to Rollan. He fell forward onto his knees, covering his ears. A long, piercing shriek ripped through the air, like a hundred thousand souls burning endlessly. Darkness blotted out the sun, and a freezing gale tore through the clearing, slicing right through Rollan's cloak and carrying ice into his bones.

Kovo began to laugh, deep, and booming, and terrifying. Rollan squinted up at him and caught a glimpse of the king as he knelt before the gorilla. The boy's hard brown eyes had changed. Now they were like the opals in his crown — shifting and luminous, but somehow blank.

Neither of them seemed to notice the screaming, the darkness, or the wind. Perhaps those were only happening in the dreamworld around the edges of the scene, but they felt horribly real to Rollan.

A huge crocodile appeared on the ground before the king, scaly and hideous and bristling with teeth. The boy reverently reached out to touch it, as if it were a glorious work of art instead of one of the ugliest, most deadly looking brutes Rollan had ever seen.

"Interesting," said Kovo. "I knew this was possible, but it's never happened before. Normally, using the Bile, you would choose an animal to bond with — but for the first time, you, my king, have summoned a true spirit animal."

"You mean — he would have come to me anyway?" the king asked.

"Yes," said Kovo. "But your bond is different because

of the Bile. Thanks to the Bile, you control him. You'll be the one in charge. Your spirit animal will do exactly as you please."

The boy king smiled in a way that Rollan didn't like at all. The wind seemed to grow stronger, more violent, ripping branches from the trees and throwing small animals off their paws.

Kovo clenched his fists and beat his chest, howling into the wind and noise and darkness.

Rollan felt certain that at any moment the gorilla would turn and attack him. But the wind was too fierce and the sound too blistering for him to move or stand or run or anything.

And then he woke up.

Or rather, Tarik woke him up, shaking his shoulder vigorously.

"Wh-what?" Rollan mumbled. He blinked, disoriented by the sudden return of the eerie, silent fog.

"You were shouting," Tarik said. "Something about monkeys."

"Gorillas," Rollan muttered. "One very big gorilla." He was lying on the ground, his head resting on a bundle that turned out to be Meilin's cloak.

"Are you all right?" Tarik asked. He crouched by Rollan's side. A small worry wrinkle had taken up permanent residence between his eyebrows.

"Yeah, just a dream," Rollan said, knowing that wasn't true. Rubbing his eyes, he sat up and twisted around until he saw Meilin.

She was sitting on a boulder with her arms folded

around her knees, staring off into the fog.

There was no sign of Jhi.

Rollan met Tarik's eyes, and the Greencloak shook his head.

"Is he awake?" Meilin called without looking back at them.

"Yes," Tarik answered.

"Then let's go," she said, hopping off the boulder.

"Go . . . ?" Rollan asked.

"Find Jhi," she said. "Silly panda probably fell asleep somewhere, like you just did." The lightness of her tone didn't match the worried look in her eyes. Rollan wasn't sure, but he suspected that she'd been crying. Now she tossed back her hair and set her jaw stubbornly. "We'll retrace our steps and—"

A shuffling sound whispered out of the fog. Meilin whirled around.

And finally, *finally*, Jhi appeared.

Her shoulders were slumped with exhaustion and her paws dragged. But when she saw Meilin, she lifted her head and a kind of light came back into her face.

"Jhi!" Meilin cried. She flung herself at the panda, wrapping her arms around Jhi's neck. Jhi sat back and put one paw around Meilin as well. For a long moment, they just leaned on each other.

Then Meilin jumped back, angrily wiping tears from her eyes. "You scared me!" she snapped. "What took you so long? Where have you been?" She shook her head. "Never mind. You're going into passive mode until we get off this island."

She started to roll up her sleeve, but the panda put a gentle paw on Meilin's hand first. Jhi indicated the fog with her other paw, tilting her head. Then she dropped to all fours and took a step away from Meilin. The expression on her face clearly said, "Well? Are you coming?"

"No," Meilin said. "Whatever you're doing, I don't want to risk you wandering off again." She held out her arm, but Rollan jumped forward.

"Wait," he said. "What if she found the conch? Maybe she's trying to lead us there."

"Is that it?" Meilin asked. "Is that where you've been?"

Jhi nodded seriously.

Rollan could see the struggle on Meilin's face. She was really afraid of losing the panda again, perhaps this time forever. He understood. When he couldn't feel Essix — well, it was horrible, as heart-wrenching and devastating as everything his mother had made him feel. That was the only way to describe it.

"Trust her," Rollan said quietly.

She shrugged him off. "All right, fine. But you stay right beside me the whole time, all right?" she ordered Jhi.

The panda nodded again, bumping Meilin's side with her own. Meilin rested her hand on the panda's back and they started walking with Rollan and Tarik close behind them.

"Um," Rollan said after a minute.

"Yes?" said Tarik.

"So . . . I'm not trying to be like Conor or anything, but . . . I had this really weird dream back there."

Tarik bowed his head, listening, as Rollan told him

about the gorilla and the king and everything he'd seen.

"What does it mean?" Rollan finished. "Conor's visions are usually telling him something. Is this a vision of the future—of something that's going to happen if Kovo gets free?"

"Or the past," Tarik mused. "This place is haunted by something that happened here long ago. Perhaps what you saw was the terrible moment that made this island the way it is?"

"I guess," Rollan said. "But how would I dream that?"

"Whatever that was, it left some powerful echoes here," Tarik said.

"It's leaving some echoes in my stomach, I can tell you that," Rollan said. He felt like he'd been turned inside out. All the weirdness of the island seemed to have crept into his blood. Dread trickled through every part of his body.

He caught himself missing Essix. She was right there on his chest, and he knew he could call her out anytime. But he also knew that as long as they were on Nightshade Island, there would be something keeping them apart.

"I hear waves," Tarik said.

A moment later, the fog shifted and they saw a beach ahead of them, with dark water slowly washing over it. They weren't exactly back where they started, but if he squinted, Rollan thought he could see the shape of their boat some ways farther along the shore.

Jhi stopped and scraped at the sand with one paw.

"Are you telling us you want to leave?" Meilin asked her, glancing out at the sea. "Because believe me, we all do. It doesn't help to waste our time with—"

A gleaming white shape began to emerge from the black sand under Jhi's paws. Rollan let out a cry of excitement and dove for it, digging away the sand. After a moment, Meilin pushed aside Jhi's clumsy paws and helped him.

It was the white conch, as luminous as a pearl and glowing in the semidarkness. Rollan carefully lifted it free, brushing away the clumps of sand in its crevices.

"Thank you, Jhi," Tarik said.

"Yes," said Rollan. "Thank you very, *very* much."

"Why would it be here, on the beach?" Meilin demanded. "All the energy of the island is in there." She waved at the dark interior.

"This has nothing to do with that," Tarik said, taking the conch from Rollan. "This only calls the Kingray, nothing more. Someone knew this island would be a good place to hide it, but my guess is they didn't want to get any closer to it than they had to. Perhaps they even threw it onshore from a boat, so they wouldn't have to set foot here."

"That's stupid," Meilin muttered.

"Doesn't matter," said Rollan. "We have it now. Let's get back to the canoe and skedaddle."

Meilin turned to Jhi with her arm outstretched, then paused. With an embarrassed glance at Rollan, she leaned forward and kissed the panda on her forehead. Putting her hands on either side of Jhi's face, she whispered, "Don't you ever scare me like that again."

The panda rubbed her nose against Meilin's, blinked, and vanished into Meilin's tattoo.

They set off toward the canoe, traipsing awkwardly

through the sand. The conch was heavy and unwieldy in Rollan's arms, and its points kept poking him sharply through his shirt.

"Did you just say 'skedaddle'?" Meilin asked Rollan after a moment.

"It is a very useful word," he said with dignity. "Your fancy tutors never taught you that one?"

"Sure they did," Meilin said. "But I have more sense than to ever use it." Rollan laughed despite himself.

But when he glanced over at her, he noticed her fingers tracing the tattoo where Jhi had disappeared. She might try not to show it, but he guessed that the island – and the feeling of losing Jhi – had deeply unsettled her.

"I hope the others are doing all right," Tarik said as he crouched to dig out the canoe.

"Are you kidding?" Rollan answered. "Where they are can't be as dangerous as this. I bet getting the black conch has been a piece of cake."

11

TRAPPED

THE TUNNEL EMERGED ONTO A HILLSIDE ONLY A FEW YARDS from one of the Conquerors' campfires. Standing across the mouth of the cave, silhouetted by the moonlight and the flickering flames, was the largest, ugliest lizard that Abeke had ever seen.

It was longer than a man, with a tail like a crocodile and thick, muscular legs that each ended in vicious-looking claws. Its forked tongue slid all the way out, nearly touching the floor, and then back in again. Scaly black-brown skin, dappled with spots of bright green, hung off it in wrinkled folds like an ill-fitting robe. It stared at her with malevolent black eyes, as though it was considering whether to eat her in one bite or two.

Abeke had a brief, wild hope that perhaps they could evade the Komodo dragon, sneak past the Conquerors' camp, and make it off the island without being spotted.

Then a huge, brawny woman with dark hair down to her knees came up behind the giant lizard and spotted them. Her eyes narrowed gleefully.

"Greencloaks!" she bellowed. "Kill them, Peleke!"

The Komodo dragon lunged at Abeke, much faster than any lizard that size should be able to move. Abeke swung her bow around, but before she could get an arrow loaded, Uraza flashed past her and leaped onto the lizard's back.

Peleke whipped around and tried to sink his jagged teeth into Uraza's leg, but she slashed at his nose and roared defiantly, leaving a trail of blood along his flat, ugly snout.

"Don't let it bite her!" Kalani shouted. "A Komodo dragon's bite is toxic!"

Abeke felt a flare of panic. She had her arrow ready, but the lizard was writhing so fast that Uraza was practically a black-and-gold blur. There was no chance of hitting Peleke without endangering the leopard. She watched helplessly as the two hissing, spitting animals rolled out of the cave entrance onto the leaf-strewn soil outside.

Meanwhile, the woman in the cave entrance had drawn two wickedly curved knives out of her sleeves. She stepped back and shouted for backup; Abeke could hear swords clattering as the warriors around the campfire leaped to their feet. In a moment, they would surround the cave, and she, Conor, and Kalani would be trapped.

"Here!" Conor shouted, grabbing Abeke's hand and shoving something into it.

Abeke glanced down and saw the Slate Elephant. She slipped the cord over her head and felt the talisman thump against her chest.

Immediately, Uraza tripled in size. The Komodo dragon

had to be at least ten feet long and probably weighed close to two hundred pounds. But now it looked like a garden lizard trapped under a house cat's paws – a really enormous house cat, that is. Uraza snarled again and slammed her front paw onto the back of the lizard's neck, slicing her claws through the tough skin and pinning it to the ground.

The Komodo dragon writhed angrily for another moment, until Abeke was able to dart forward and finish it off with an arrow.

"Run!" Conor shouted.

They pelted out of the cave and swerved away from the campfire, running downhill in the opposite direction. Behind them, Abeke heard Uraza roaring and batting Conquerors away like balls of yarn. She felt the leopard's sinuous strength flowing through her as she hurtled past fallen branches and vaulted over mossy boulders. She smelled the salt tang of the ocean up ahead and veered toward it, even as she also felt Uraza's instinctive shudder of horror at getting any closer to the sea.

They burst out of the trees onto the beach: Abeke, then Briggan and Conor with the enormous conch, then Kalani.

"This way!" Kalani shouted, running toward the cove where they'd hidden their canoe.

Abeke looked back, catching her breath, and saw the tops of the trees thrashing frantically as giant Uraza came barreling down the slope after them. She could hear the clangs and shouts of more Conquerors in pursuit.

"Come on, Uraza!" she shouted. There was no time now for caution or stealth. They had to run, and hope against hope that they could outrun an entire island full of Conquerors and their monstrous beasts.

The giant leopard leaped onto the beach and yowled angrily as sand sprayed up her nose and along her whiskers. Abeke turned to run, but Uraza yowled again and grabbed at Abeke's cloak with one front paw.

Abeke guessed what she was trying to say, and although they'd never done anything like this before, she somehow knew exactly how to clamber up Uraza's leg and where to sit between her shoulders. She leaned forward, burying her face and fists in the leopard's thick fur, and held on for dear life as Uraza rocketed down the beach.

Once, when Abeke was about seven years old, she'd ridden on a camel. She remembered that it was uncomfortable and high and scary, that the camel had rolled alarmingly from side to side as it walked, that it had made awful spitting noises at her, and that Soama had laughed when Abeke cried that she wanted to get off.

This was *nothing* at all like riding a camel.

This was speed and smooth power and pure joy, and if they weren't being chased by a horde of murderous enemies, Abeke would have been happy to keep running like this forever.

She leaned down and called to her friends as Uraza sped toward them.

"Here, climb up!" she shouted, holding out one arm.

"You'll be faster without us!" Kalani shouted back. "Go on ahead and get the boat ready! We'll be right behind you!"

Abeke realized that made sense; they needed to get to their boat before the Conquerors found it. She threw her arms back around the leopard's neck and they flew past

Conor and Kalani, reaching the cove first.

So Abeke was the first to see that their carefully constructed hideout of rocks and branches had been dismantled . . . and their canoe was gone.

Standing in its place was a guard of twelve armed Conquerors.

"No!" Abeke shouted, yanking back on Uraza's fur without thinking about it. The leopard skidded to a stop and let out a snarl that shook the trees. She crouched as though she were about to pounce.

"Uraza, wait," Abeke cried. "Go back to Conor and Kalani. This is a trap!"

The leopard growled again, but she stepped back. The Conquerors were already running forward, notching arrows into bows and pulling out throwing knives.

Abeke gripped Uraza's back with her knees and pulled out her own bow. As the leopard turned and ran back to the beach, Abeke twisted around and fired arrow after arrow into the Conquerors' midst. She saw a vicious-looking wild boar go down with a loud squeal. Another arrow struck a bearded man in the shoulder, and he staggered to his knees.

A squawk sounded overhead and Abeke whipped her bow up in time to fire at an attacking seagull just before it dove at her head. She missed, but it shrieked at her and soared away. She wondered if it was the same one who'd tried to steal the talisman from Conor on the ship. The Slate Elephant bumped against her collarbone, a tempting target for any ambitious attackers.

The Conquerors fell back to regroup behind a wall of

rocks as Uraza reached Conor, Briggan, and Kalani.

"The canoe is gone," Abeke panted, sliding off Uraza's back.

Conor went white. "How are we going to get off this island?" he said. "Steal one of their boats? They'll have thought of that," he answered himself. "They'll be waiting for us, wherever their boats are."

"I have a better idea," Kalani said. "If you don't mind getting wet – and you don't mind me borrowing that." She pointed at the Slate Elephant.

"Oh," Conor said doubtfully. "Uh – do you think that will work? I'm . . . not the world's best swimmer."

"You don't have to be," Kalani said. "Katoa and I will take care of you."

"It's our best chance," Abeke agreed. She pulled the talisman off her neck and Uraza shrank to her usual, still-quite-intimidating size. Then she handed it to Kalani, who put it on reverently and waded straight into the ocean.

Conor and Abeke held out their arms; Briggan and Uraza vanished, and almost at the same moment, Kalani's dolphin appeared. Only now the dolphin was much, much bigger than when they'd first seen him.

Abeke eyed the dolphin's smooth, rubbery skin anxiously. There was no fur to hold on to here. Kalani was used to riding him, but how would Conor and Abeke stay on?

The dolphin caught Abeke's eye and smiled. At least, it looked like a smile – a genuine, trust-me, don't-worry, this'll-be-fun smile. He flipped his tail and splashed them all.

"Come on," Kalani said.

Abeke heard voices shouting along the beach. The Conquerors had figured out their plan. There was no more time to lose.

She hurried into the water, paddling the last few feet as the seafloor dipped out of sight below her. Conor flailed and splashed along behind her, still clutching the black conch under his arm.

Kalani was already on Katoa's back; she reached down and hauled Abeke up behind her. The dolphin felt slippery and cool under Abeke's hands as she wriggled into a sitting position. "Just hang on to me!" Kalani called. Abeke wrapped her arms around the older girl's waist as Kalani dragged Conor onto the dolphin in front of her. He tucked his cloak around the conch in his arms, closed his eyes, and curled into the dolphin with a look of dread on his face.

Abeke held her breath as the giant dolphin plunged into the waves. Salt water stung her nose and throat as they submerged, then came up to the surface again. Conor coughed and sputtered frantically. Abeke clung to Kalani for dear life.

At first it was terrifying, like she was seven all over again, but after a minute she got used to the rise and fall of the dolphin's back between her knees and the way the ocean swept over them each time they went under. It started to feel exhilarating, like leaping through clouds. She took a deep breath in, letting relief sweep through her.

When Abeke twisted around to look back, she saw Sunlight Island rapidly shrinking into the distance. Even as the Conquerors ran for boats to follow them, it was clear they'd never catch up.

Thanks to Katoa and Kalani, she and Conor had gotten the black conch and escaped safely.

Now they just had to hope that Rollan and Meilin had been successful too — and then they could call the Kingray and finally be on their way to Mulop.

12

ANOTHER DREAM

MEILIN STOOD ON THE RUINS OF A BRIDGE IN A DESOLATE garden, gazing down into the empty ponds below her. The pale orange and white bodies of large, once-beautiful fish lay tangled in the rotting mass of greenery.

All around her, the trees and flowering plants were dead, their lifeless wet branches drooping and broken or flattened pathetically to the ground.

The whole garden looked drowned, as if a tsunami had come through, destroyed everything, and then stormed back into the ocean.

Grandfather Xao's garden.

She still recognized it, even in this state. She could imagine how her grandparents would shriek at the sight of it, after all the meticulous work they'd done to the place over the years. They would be furious—for five minutes. Then they would roll up their sleeves and start cleaning it up.

Meilin set aside the parasol she was holding, crouched,

and started pulling weeds out of the cracks in the bridge's boards, tossing them down into the pond under her.

"Don't waste your energy, Tiny Tiger."

Meilin scrambled to her feet and whirled around.

Her father stepped up onto the bridge, staring out into the garden with grief in his eyes. "I loved this place. I loved it as a child, and I loved bringing you here when you were small." He flashed a sad smile at her. "It was one of the few places you ever had a chance to play. You've had to grow up so fast, Meilin."

"Father," Meilin choked out. He looked . . . healthy, strong, powerful. Alive.

Something moved in the overgrown bushes behind him. Meilin tensed and reached for the parasol – but it wasn't a parasol anymore. It was a spear, the end wickedly sharp and gleaming.

Then Jhi stepped out of the greenery and looked around, blinking slowly. Her silver eyes met Meilin's and she came padding up onto the bridge. Meilin's father looked down at the panda as she passed him.

"A terrible mistake," he murmured.

"She's not," Meilin said. "I thought so at first, but . . . we are meant for each other."

Jhi stood up on her hind legs and rested her front paws on the shattered railing of the bridge. The black fur around her eyes made them seem even larger and sadder. "I hope you always remember that, Meilin," she said in a velvety voice.

A sense of foreboding shivered across Meilin's skin. Up in the sky, a flock of ravens erupted from one of the dead trees and scattered across the gray clouds, cawing harshly.

"Get out!" her father shouted abruptly. Meilin jumped, terrified by the anger in his voice. He took a step toward Meilin and stared furiously into her eyes. "Get out!" he shouted again. "You're not my daughter!"

Meilin stumbled back, nearly falling through a spot where the wood of the bridge had rotted completely away.

"I am!" she cried. "Father, what's wrong?"

Blood began to bubble out from between his lips. To her horror, Meilin saw more patches of blood spreading all across his chest, seeping through his robe. "I never should have listened to you!" he hissed.

"I'm sorry," Meilin said, her voice trembling. "Father, please." But he shoved away her outstretched hands and turned his back on her. His back, too, was bleeding from a hundred wounds, many of them the size and shape of giant crocodile teeth.

"Don't touch me," he growled. "You're not my daughter."

It began to rain, the kind of cold, dripping, mind-numbing rain you'd expect to symbolize misery in a dream.

"Jhi," Meilin pleaded, turning to her spirit animal. "What's wrong with him? Why is he so angry at me?" She buried her face in her hands. "Because I got him killed, is that why?"

"Meilin," said the panda. Jhi came up beside Meilin, pressing her warm bulk against the girl's side. "Forgive yourself. Now, and then, and later."

"I can't," Meilin whispered through her tears.

"There is worse to come," Jhi warned softly.

"Worse than losing my father and all of Zhong?" Meilin

asked. General Teng started to limp away, clutching his side and stopping for breath every few minutes. All she wanted was to run after him and have him fold her in his arms, the way he used to when she was small.

But the fury in his eyes . . . She couldn't face it again.

"Worse," murmured Jhi. "Oh, Meilin . . . I can't tell you, but you need to know. . . ."

Her voice trailed off as a freezing wind began to sweep through the garden.

"What is it?" Meilin asked. "What's going to happen?"

Jhi leaned forward as though she was trying to speak, but the wind, and rain, and rattling dead branches drowned out her voice. Meilin crouched and put her hands on either side of Jhi's face, bringing them nose to nose. But she still couldn't hear anything Jhi said. Whatever warning the panda was trying to deliver, it couldn't get through.

All Meilin could see was herself reflected in Jhi's silver eyes: a girl with no father and no home, a girl who couldn't trust anyone. A girl who had to save Erdas with nothing but a panda.

Meilin closed her eyes and rested her forehead against Jhi's soft black-and-white fur.

When she opened them again, Jhi was gone and Meilin was back in the canoe, rocking on the waves. The sky was the lavender of her handmaiden Kusha's favorite silk kimono; a few stars were just beginning to glimmer above her as the sun set. Her legs ached and her arms felt like they were full of small needles. She realized she'd had her face pressed against her spirit animal tattoo as she slept.

She sat up, rubbing her upper arms, and Rollan pulled

his paddle in and twisted around to look at her.

"I'm glad you got some sleep," he said. "It looked like you needed it."

Meilin didn't answer. She would have chosen to go without sleep for a week if she could have avoided that dream.

Now it would haunt her forever: her father's bloodied face shouting "Get out!" and "You're not my daughter!" surrounded by the wreckage of her childhood.

She curled her arms around her legs and closed her eyes, determined not to cry.

It was just a dream.

Except the last time she'd spoken to Jhi in a dream, the panda had helped her wake up to realize she was sleepwalking in the rain on Sunset Tower.

So what did this dream mean?

Was something terrible about to happen?

What was Jhi trying to tell her?

13

THE KINGRAY

DAGGER POINT TURNED OUT TO BE A LONG, NARROW PENINsula ending in a chain of sharper and sharper rocks that jutted into the sea like it was knifing it. It was the northernmost point of the southernmost island in the Hundred Isles, and in places the cool blue sea was so calm and the reflections of the clouds so clear that it looked as if you'd be leaping right into the sky if you dove in.

Of course, Rollan had no intention of doing any such thing.

He was a sensible person who would keep his boots on land as much as possible, thank you very much. Unlike some people, who were evidently comfortable gallivanting around the ocean on giant dolphins.

He squinted at Conor and Abeke as Kalani's dolphin swam up to the shore, and revised that assessment. Conor looked anything *but* comfortable.

The good news, though, was that as Conor wobbled off the side of the dolphin and floundered ashore with Abeke and Kalani's help, Rollan caught a clear glimpse of the black conch in his arms.

"They did it," he said to Meilin. She was standing on the sharpest rock at the end of the daggerlike archipelago, hands on her hips, staring out to sea with the wind tossing her dark ponytail.

"Of course they did," she said without turning around.

"Has anyone ever told you that your trust issues are all over the place?" Rollan asked.

She just snorted in response.

Lenori was on the beach, next to the canoe she'd brought and the ashes of the *tapu*-touched canoe they'd had to burn. She waited as the others staggered through the waves. They were too far away to hear, but Rollan saw her step forward and say something to Kalani. The young queen flinched back and made a sign with her hands in the direction of Dagger Point. In the direction of Rollan and Meilin.

And Tarik, who stood behind him. Tarik put one hand on Rollan's shoulder.

"She's warding off evil," he explained simply.

"Great," Rollan said. "We step on one haunted island and suddenly we're evil?"

"You felt that place," Tarik said. "You know it's more than superstition; they're right to fear it. We can't burden Kalani with the weight of *tapu*. She has her whole tribe to think of. She's better off staying away from us."

Rollan tilted his head back to watch Essix soaring in high, swooping circles far overhead. He just knew he never wanted to go back to Nightshade Island ever again. And if he could shake the nightmare of staring into Kovo's malevolent eyes, that would be great too.

"Bye," he heard Meilin whisper. He followed her gaze to where Kalani and her dolphin – now back to its regular size – were swimming away. He wondered if the young queen would be able to keep her people safe with so many Conquerors so close by.

Conor echoed that thought as he climbed out over the long rocks toward them. Rollan could hear him asking Lenori, "But won't the Conquerors know it was her who helped us? What if they punish her?"

"Kalani is a wise and strong queen," Lenori assured him. "She will protect them as long as she can." The rest of the thought was left unspoken, but Rollan could finish it in his head: *The best way to help her is to stop the Devourer once and for all.*

Rollan reached out a hand to help Conor hop onto the rock next to him.

Conor grinned his thanks. "I understand you guys are all touched by the spirit of darkness now or something."

"No joke," Rollan said. "I might accidentally kill you in my sleep."

Conor's smile faltered, and Rollan realized that it wasn't at all funny, with an actual mole in their midst somewhere who might one day try to do exactly that.

"Sorry," he said. "Just kidding. Um . . . so how was Sunlight Island?"

"A little terrifying," Conor admitted. "But Abeke and Uraza were amazing."

"Conor's the one who found the conch," Abeke said, and they exchanged a smile.

Wish I could say we had a bonding experience too, Rollan thought. *But it was kind of more of an* un-*bonding experience.* Then again, he remembered the curl of Meilin's fingers between his, and her slender, strong shoulders leaning into his arm. He wasn't actually sure if they were closer or further apart than ever right now. She'd barely said more than five words since they left Nightshade Island, even when he'd tried saying some deliberately stupid things to provoke her into teasing him.

As if his thought had summoned her, Meilin turned and balanced her way back along the rocks toward them, hopping gracefully like a jungle cat.

Abeke frowned and ducked her head to peer into Meilin's face. "Are you all right?" she asked.

"Why wouldn't I be?" Meilin snapped.

"You just – sorry, you look – you just look like you've seen a ghost, or – more like a ghost has cut off one of your arms or something. So I just thought – if you want to talk about it –"

That was eerily close, Rollan thought. He remembered someone saying once that losing a spirit animal was worse than losing a limb. He flexed his hand and looked up to check on Essix again.

Meilin gave Abeke a withering look. "I don't have anything I need to talk about with *you*," she said. "Or with *anyone* here." She glared around at Tarik, Conor, Lenori, and Rollan. "Nobody wants to say it, but we all know that one of us is the mole. One of us has been helping the enemy. Somebody here has been telling them how to find us—which means somebody here led the Conquerors right to us in Zhong. Whoever the mole is—" She looked straight at Abeke. "*That's* the person who killed my father."

"Meilin—" Tarik said quietly. Abeke looked as if she'd been stabbed.

"So no, I don't want to have a heartfelt conversation about our *feelings*," Meilin went on. "I want to call this Kingray, get the Coral Octopus, and finish this stupid quest before the Conquerors catch up to us yet again." She snatched the white conch out of Rollan's hands and snapped her fingers twice at Conor. "Ready?"

"Um." He fumbled with the black conch for a moment, then finally raised it to his mouth and nodded.

Meilin drew a deep breath, and together they blew a long, resonant, rolling sound across the waves. The tone of the black conch was higher than that of the white conch, but they blended together like eerie music. The notes reverberated in Rollan's ears and seemed to echo across the water long after Meilin and Conor finally lowered the seashells.

Nothing happened for several minutes.

"Didn't it work?" Meilin asked Lenori impatiently. "Did we do it wrong?"

Lenori spread her hands with that infinitely serene expression of hers, which Rollan was fairly certain was Meilin's least favorite expression in Lenori's repertoire.

But before they could start to argue, Rollan spotted a strange ripple in the sea—like a wave going the wrong way, cutting across the other, regular waves.

"There!" he cried, pointing.

It was definitely coming toward them.

"Is it the Kingray?" Abeke asked.

"I'm guessing yes," Rollan said, "unless there happen to be a lot of comically oversized stingrays around these parts."

He was joking, but the flat, rippling creature coming toward them gave him the definite heebie-jeebies. Its edges flowed like banners moving in the wind. It had nothing that could be called a head or limbs. Strange black eyes peered at them from the top of the flat surface, and a long, thin tail like a pointed stick jutted out the back.

And *huge* didn't seem like quite the word for it. It was massive, like a large gray raft. *Gray* wasn't the right description for its color either: something else, somewhere between dark green and violet and sand with freckles of russet red and splashes of brown. It was not a normal color.

It was not a normal animal.

The Kingray slowed to a stop in front of them and floated there in the water. Like an underwater flying carpet, just waiting for them to step aboard.

"That is a big—that is a weird—I don't even—" Rollan ran out of half-sentences. There was really no part of him, not even the tiniest hidden small corner, that wanted to climb on board the world's most enormous stingray.

"We're really supposed to ride it?" Conor asked Tarik.

"There's nothing to hang on to," Rollan pointed out.

"And it's not big enough for all six of us," Meilin added. "Four at the most." She stepped forward. "Well, *I'm* not staying here." She crouched and rested one foot lightly on the Kingray's back. When it didn't move, she shifted her weight forward and then stepped all the way onto it.

The Kingray sank a few inches and rippled quietly, unconcerned.

"No worse than riding a rockback whale surrounded by sharks," Meilin said, and Rollan thought he saw a glimmer of her usual teasing spirit in her eyes. "But of course, Rollan, if you're too *scared* to ride a giant stingray, you could always stay here. . . ."

"I'm not scared," he protested. "I just think it would be more sensible to take, say, a boat, and maybe follow the Kingray wherever it's going."

They all looked at the Kingray for a reaction to this. There was none. It continued to ripple quietly. Rollan found himself appreciating the fact that at least his spirit animal had a face. If someone bonded with a stingray, how would they ever know what it was thinking? At least Essix could use her face – and beak, and talons, and piercing voice – to make her emotions quite clear.

"I don't think a boat could keep up with the Kingray," Abeke guessed. "You saw how fast it traveled. That's probably part of the point – since only the Kingray knows how to get to Mulop, this way only a limited number of people can visit him at once."

Lenori nodded. "That does make sense. He's a private octopus."

Rollan bit back a laugh. A year ago, racing through the streets of Concorba, surviving on scraps and arguing over nicknames with his former friends, Rollan could never in his life have expected to hear someone say "he's a private octopus" with such grave intensity.

"It should be the four of us," Conor said. "The Four Fallen. That's who Mulop wants to see." He turned to Tarik. "You get the ship and the whales ready to leave. We'll go get the talisman."

"No," Tarik said, stepping forward with a determined expression. "I can't send you all off into the ocean – into the entire wide-open *ocean*, to any of a *hundred* islands – with no idea of where you're going or whether it's safe. What kind of protector would do that? Hand you over to a giant stingray, with no way to find you if you don't come back? If anything happened to any of the Four Fallen . . . if anything happened to any of *you* . . . it would – I couldn't –"

He broke off, shaking his head. There was a moment of strange quiet. None of them had ever seen Tarik so emotional.

"Oh, Tarik," Lenori said sympathetically. "You're starting to sound like a worried father. I understand that you care about them; we both do. But they're not ordinary children, and in this case they're right. Mulop wants to see the Four Fallen."

"Well, he can see three of the Fallen and me," Tarik said stubbornly.

"Really?" Meilin challenged him. "Which one of us would *you* leave behind?"

Tarik looked at each of them in turn, unhappiness written in deep lines across his face. Rollan could hear the unspoken question underneath Meilin's. *Who do you think is the mole? Which of us do you trust the least?*

After all this time traveling with Tarik, Rollan knew him well enough to know he would never answer that question. It would devastate whomever he chose, and Tarik was too protective to do that, even if he did have his own private suspicions.

"We'll be careful, Tarik," Conor promised. "This is the only way to get the talisman."

"I agree," said Lenori. She pushed back the folds of her green cloak and put her hands to her temples, closing her eyes as though she was trying to remember her dreams. "I'm sorry, Tarik, but in every one of my visions, I've seen all four of the Fallen—Jhi, Uraza, Briggan, and Essix. I'm afraid if any of them don't show up, Mulop may decide not to help us. Can we risk losing this talisman?"

"Isn't it worse to risk losing Meilin, Abeke, Conor, or Rollan?" Tarik demanded. "Or all of them at once? Sometimes . . . sometimes I wonder if Barlow was right, Lenori. We ask so much of them so young. Ordinary or not, they *are* children."

Rollan remembered Barlow, the former Greencloak they'd met on their very first quest through the mountains of Amaya. Barlow didn't like that the Greencloaks recruited kids, and he'd said as much to Tarik.

Had Tarik been carrying that same worry around all this time?

"Mulop is not dangerous like Cabaro or Dinesh," Lenori insisted. "He's friendly to our cause, and we should keep him that way."

"Besides," Rollan pointed out, "the mole can't betray us this time, because none of us know where we're going.

Right? That's the upside of being a secret location – the bad guys can't find it either." He nudged Tarik's arm.

There was a sort of awkward pause, as if everyone else had been worrying about the mole too, but trying not to bring it up.

Abeke nodded. "It's really all right, Tarik. You've taught us well. We can take care of each other, and we'll be back soon."

Tarik rubbed his face with a furious movement. "I can feel that this is wrong," he said. "I'm no seer, but I've been in more than a few battles and there's a sense you get when things aren't right. Lumeo is anxious too. Don't any of you feel it? I fear that something awful is about to happen."

"That's just your worry talking," Meilin said, shifting impatiently. Her hand went to the tattoo of Jhi, and she bit her lip.

"Yeah, it sounds kind of like how I feel all the time," Rollan tried to joke. He'd never seen the elder Greencloak so nervous. Usually Tarik was cool and collected – a force of calm even when things looked bad. If even stone-faced Tarik was scared, shouldn't the rest of them be?

"Have faith in us," Conor said with a smile. He held out his hand for Tarik to shake.

The Greencloak still looked unhappy and unconvinced. Slowly he took Conor's hand. "Promise me you'll be careful. Promise me you'll come back."

"Of course," Conor said.

"We promise," Abeke added, and Rollan and Meilin nodded too.

Tarik sighed and dropped Conor's hand. "Here's the

Granite Ram," he said, handing it to Rollan. "I hope it helps you."

"And I have the Slate Elephant," Abeke said, touching her pocket.

"Don't worry about us," Meilin said. "We'll be back soon."

Tarik reached up to his shoulder and gathered Lumeo in his hands, as if he needed something to hold on to.

Abeke was already climbing down onto the stingray. Rollan couldn't stand around like a coward any longer. He scrambled over the rocks until he could lower his feet onto the ray's back. Like Meilin, he carefully leaned his weight forward, then stood up – and promptly slipped and fell right into the ocean.

Meilin reached in and hauled him back out. "Idiot," she said, but he thought he detected a note of affection in there.

"Just testing the water," he said. "Nice and warm. Much warmer than – ah, than the last time I got dunked." That was in Eura, when that brutish walrus had stolen the Crystal Polar Bear.

Conor joined them, crouching next to Abeke, who'd seated herself cross-legged. Rollan sat on her other side, as close to the middle of the ray as he could get. Its back felt weird and rubbery under his fingers, with an odd prickly texture when he swept his hand in the wrong direction, but smooth as skin in the other.

It was also extremely wet. The Kingray was floating just below the surface of the water, and sank slightly as they each climbed on, so they were all partially submerged by the time everyone was on board. Seawater sloshed around their legs and soaked their pants.

Abeke brushed her leopard tattoo with her fingers. "Uraza would hate this," she said.

Meilin glanced down at them, as if she was considering trying to stay upright for the ride. But finally she sat down as well, wrinkling her nose and wrapping her cloak up around her shoulders to keep it dry.

The moment she was seated, the Kingray began to move, rippling forward and out into the open ocean.

"Good luck!" Tarik called anxiously. "Please be safe!" Lenori was right; the elder Greencloak sounded more like a parent than a guardian. Rollan felt a strange tug of concern. He wasn't sure if it was just Tarik's worry spreading to him, but suddenly the sky seemed heavy above them. Why did this parting feel so final?

Rollan waved good-bye as Dagger Point, Lenori, and Tarik rapidly shrank to tiny shapes behind them. He was surprised to realize how much he wished Tarik could have come with them after all. He tilted his head back to make sure Essix was still above them, following the Kingray, although he didn't really need to look to know that. He could sense her there, all the more keenly now that the experience on Nightshade Island had let him know what a giant empty hole would be left in his chest without her.

The ocean flew past in a blue-green blur, with white sprays of water pluming on either side of them. From the ship, Rollan had looked out at Oceanus and thought it was a sunny, beautiful place. He didn't know anyone who'd ever spent time playing or relaxing on a beach, but he'd heard that it was something the wealthy of Concorba would travel miles to do. He'd never understood that — why roll around in sand and deal with roaring, moving water if you didn't have to?

Seeing the beaches of Oceanus had given him a glimpse of the appeal. He'd now traveled across almost the entire world of Erdas, and these islands were possibly the most beautiful of any of the places they'd visited.

But the view from the deck of a ship was quite different from the view on top of a giant stingray.

The sparkling, glassy turquoise waters turned out to be teeming with life, and it was even more visible to Rollan with the extra-sharp eyesight that came from his bond with Essix. Countless fish in every color of the rainbow swam below them, including several of the large silver ones that Rollan remembered seeing in the fish traps they'd waded past in the harbor of Xin Kao Dai. None of the sea life seemed afraid of the Kingray; many of the fish came close enough for Rollan to touch, if he wanted to risk leaning over the side to try.

One school of thin lemon-yellow fish darted by, each of them as long as his arm. Far below them, on the sandy ocean floor, Rollan spotted a huge starfish with stubby teeth-like ridges along its five arms; it glowed the same amber color as Essix's eyes.

As long as he remained seated, it was easier than he would have expected to stay on the Kingray. Rollan had half imagined that he'd go flying off the minute it moved, but they sped along smoothly. It was almost no different than sitting on a floor, apart from the wind rushing through his hair and the water spraying his face.

He had a strange flash of a memory—something he hadn't thought about in years. In it, he was very small, and his mother was there. She'd set him on a scrap of red-and-gold carpet and then pulled him around the room like it was a sled, faster and faster, whirling and laughing. He remembered her laughing face, eyes shining at him. He remembered giggling until he fell off the carpet, over and over again.

That must have been one of her rare good days. He hadn't thought he had any happy memories of her.

Much good it does me, he thought savagely. *She's the Devourer's slave now, controlled by the Bile. Even if I did want my mother back, I couldn't have her.*

He felt something brush his knee and looked up into Meilin's eyes. The wind had flung away the cord she usually used to tie up her hair, and now it flew in a wild dark cloud around her head. When he'd met her, he'd been struck by her beauty, but now when he looked at her he saw so much more—her unbelievable fighting skills, her intelligence, her sharp humor, her steely strength.

I'm glad it was me that Essix chose, he realized. *I'm glad it was me, and I'm glad Jhi chose her.*

Meilin touched his knee again and tilted her head, as if she'd seen some of his struggle in his face, but she didn't want to intrude by asking.

"Nothing important," he said, answering her unspoken question. "Just . . . thinking about Aidana."

"Maybe there's a way to set her free," she said. "If there is, I promise you we'll find it."

He nodded, not quite ready yet to let himself hope. His gaze shifted back to the water, where he could now see a coral reef not far off to their left, bright pinks and purples and oranges in the shapes of strange frozen plants. The whole thing shimmered with the movement of hundreds of sea creatures, darting in and out of the small holes or crawling along the outside of the coral.

"Look," Abeke said in a breathless voice. She pointed to something swimming up ahead of them — lots of somethings, parts of them surfacing and submerging as they swam.

"Sharks?" Conor asked nervously.

"No," Meilin said, cracking her first smile since Nightshade Island. "Seals."

The Kingray sailed smoothly right through the pod of seals; they parted to let it by as quickly and neatly as street urchins scattering before a carriage in the city. Sleek brown heads popped out of the water to watch them go by. Rollan grinned at the curious, almost puzzled expressions on their whiskered faces. Their eyes were huge and brown and surprisingly human, a lot like the baby orangutan's. Most of them had rolls of fat under their necks like double chins, making them look even sillier.

With a twinge of guilt, Rollan thought of the seal hunt they'd witnessed with the Ardu in Arctica. These seals looked smaller and sleeker than those, gleaming like oiled wood under the water. *They'd understand, though*, he told himself. *They have to eat to survive too, just like the Ardu hunters.*

Three of the seals — the smallest and therefore perhaps

the youngest and the bravest—followed the Kingray for as long as they could keep up. They kept darting under the Kingray and popping up on the other side, then flipping their tails to splash the riders and ducking under again.

"They're trying to play with us," Abeke said, delighted.

"They kind of remind me of Lumeo," Conor said. "Or some of the puppies we had when I was a kid." He waved at the closest seal and it whacked the water with one of its flippers, its eyes sparkling mischievously.

Rollan twisted to watch the seals vanish under the water as the Kingray pulled away from them. He wondered if he and his friends would survive long enough to see a day when they could just enjoy a place like this—the sunshine, swimming with the seals, the warm water. He could almost, but not quite, imagine what it would be like if they didn't have the darkness of the Devourer hanging over them and the weight of Erdas's future in their hands.

"Are we slowing down?" Conor asked.

Rollan dipped his fingertips in the ocean and watched the ripples flow past. "I think so," he said. He squinted up in the direction the Kingray was swimming. "Does that mean that's where we're going?"

They all turned to look at the island that was coming closer and closer. Rollan had expected something majestic and weird for the home of a Great Beast—an entire palace made of seaweed, perhaps. But this was a perfectly ordinary-looking island, perhaps a bit more rocky and bare than the other ninety-nine that made up the Hundred Isles. There was nothing extraordinary about it at all.

But this was clearly their destination. The only landing spot was a crescent-shaped cove with a white sand beach; tall cliffs of rock made up the other sides of the island, knobbed and pockmarked and rough like a coral reef. The Kingray gradually slowed more and more until it floated solemnly into the cove and flared to a stop in shallow water.

"This is it?" Rollan asked the giant stingray.

"Where's Mulop?" Meilin demanded. They could see pretty much the whole island from where they were, and there was certainly nothing that looked like a giant octopus.

The Kingray, predictably, did not answer.

"I guess that's our cue to start looking," Conor said cheerfully. He rolled off into the waves and splashed over to the beach. Two reddish-orange crabs the size of Rollan's hand saw Conor coming and scuttled away sideways into their holes. They vanished just as Briggan appeared from Conor's tattoo and bounded onto the sand. The wolf shook himself vigorously and started galloping up and down the beach like a puppy finally let into the sunshine after a rainy day.

"Maybe Mulop is underwater?" Abeke guessed. She scooted off the Kingray, peering into the sapphire blue sea as she jumped in. Apart from the clouds of sand kicked up by Conor as he'd gone ashore, the water was clear enough to see the ocean floor for a long way in each direction. Nothing there looked like a giant octopus either, or like the entrance to a giant octopus's secret lair.

Rollan felt a flicker of intuition stirring in his brain.

He looked up at Essix, soaring overhead, and felt it again, even stronger. They *were* close to Mulop. But they wouldn't find him down on the beach – they had to climb up the rocks to the cliffs and search there, as odd as that seemed.

Nobody argued with him, though, when he and Meilin reached the sand and he told them what he'd felt.

"All right," Conor said. "Let's climb."

"Are you going to wait for us?" Meilin asked the Kingray. "Float there unhelpfully like a wet piece of silk if the answer is yes."

The Kingray stared impassively at her, rippling quietly.

"That better be a yes," Rollan said. "I really do not want to get stuck here."

Essix came soaring down and landed suddenly on his shoulder. Her talons gently squeezed and she nibbled at his hair with her beak.

"Can you help us find Mulop?" he asked her.

She clacked her beak and he felt it again, like something physically tugging him up the rocks. He followed the sensation, leading the way up until they reached the top of the island cliffs. There were no trees up here, nothing but a flat tabletop of stone and a view out to distant green-and-white islands.

Except for one thing: a great wide hole in the stone, yawning and dark like an open mouth.

Rollan immediately regretted having that thought. Because the only thing to do, the obvious thing to do, was to climb down into it.

He pulled out the Granite Ram, remembering Tarik's

worried face as the Greencloak handed it to him. "I'll go first," he offered. He slipped the talisman around his neck and swung his legs into the hole. It wasn't a straight dark shaft after all; he immediately felt a ledge below his feet, and then he saw boulders strewn about all the way down, and light glowing at the bottom.

As he climbed down, the Granite Ram helped him leap lightly from one boulder to the next, keeping his feet even as the rocks became wetter and more slippery. It became brighter and brighter the farther down he went, and soon he realized that there were other holes in the walls, allowing sunlight to filter into the cavern.

Finally he felt solid ground underfoot and stopped, looking around him for the first time. He found himself standing on a lip of rock in an underground grotto, facing a vast hidden lake. Small, murmuring waves lapped at his feet. The air was damp but smelled fresh and clean, like the sky after a rainstorm.

Emerald green sunbeams poured down through a hundred small holes in the rocks overhead, while at the same time an eerie, radiantly blue light glowed from under the water itself. Rollan felt like he was standing inside a piece of sea glass.

He heard scrambling noises overhead and turned, climbing back up the rocks a ways until he could pass the Granite Ram to the others.

They each slid down next to him, Meilin and then Conor and Briggan, and then Abeke, and stared around with startled eyes.

"It's beautiful," Abeke whispered, but even that small

sound echoed off the high ceilings and came murmuring back to them.

"Yes," said a new voice, dark and rich and somehow full of bubbles. "I've always thought so too."

Rollan felt Meilin seize his hand and grip it tightly.

A shape was rising out of the water: the shape of the largest octopus the world had ever seen.

They'd found Mulop, at last.

14

MULOP

THE OCTOPUS REGARDED THEM FOR A LONG MOMENT, DURING which Conor found himself completely unable to speak. Mulop's bulbous dark orange head nearly touched the rocks overhead, and yet there was obviously a lot more of him still hidden underwater. He looked like a giant brain on top of a pair of eyes on top of a web of tentacles, and that was it. His expression was completely unreadable. Angry? Bemused? Delighted? Half asleep? Conor had no idea.

"Hmm," Mulop said at length. A long, purplish-orange tentacle snaked out of the water and poked at Briggan, who had scrambled down the rocks behind Conor. The wolf sniffed at the tentacle and sneezed, but stayed still as it drifted over his fur and tail and paws.

"Smaller than I remember," mused Mulop. Conor couldn't see a mouth—he couldn't see anything but enormous deep green eyes in that huge dark orange head—but as with the other Great Beasts, he seemed to hear the octopus's voice inside his head as well as echoing throughout the cavern.

"Is this what I remember?" Mulop asked thoughtfully. "No, I'm right, he was bigger before."

Briggan yipped, as if defending himself.

"Yes, yes," Mulop said. "Time to grow. Certainly, if there is time, and space for growing, and giant wolfishness to grow into, anyone could, perhaps."

The tentacle moved suddenly to Conor, wrapping around his whole body and then patting his face. Rubbery suction cups squished against his cheeks and brushed his eyelashes. He held his breath, trying to appear infinitely braver than he actually felt.

"Hmm," Mulop said again. "Also smaller than I expected." The tentacle tapped his nose and then poked him in the stomach, nearly knocking the breath from him. "Thought they came bigger than this, didn't I? I certainly did. Remember the tall ones from last time? True, still rather small, but not this small. Less time to grow here, but some. Also mute? Very unexpected. Did I expect that? No, I did not."

"I'm not mute," Conor blurted.

The tentacle patted his face again, and he got a strong impression that Mulop was pleased.

"Excellent," said the octopus. His voice was quiet but had an echoing quality to it, and a bass note like it was being pulled up from the far depths of the ocean. "Won't that make things easier? It will, I'm right. I prefer questions, don't I? Yes, otherwise it's hard to keep track of what I know and others don't know, and there's so much

I know and everyone else doesn't know, but then it's not surprising when I know so much, after all. Oh, I have a question. Go ahead." He paused, and Conor thought for a moment that Mulop was waiting for him to speak, but then the octopus sailed right on. "Where are my other friends? Ah, good question. I think they're here, don't I? Indeed."

It's like he's talking to himself, Conor realized. He wondered if it was lonely, being the only underwater Great Beast. Perhaps Mulop talked to himself because there was usually no one else to talk to.

The tentacle let go of Conor and moved on to prod the others, one at a time. "Friends? Friends? Are you in there? Don't be shy. Do I think they're being shy? That certainly doesn't sound like them. Uraza was never – aha!" The huge octopus's eyes lit up with delight as Jhi appeared on the ledge beside Meilin. "Oh, panda panda panda. Unnaturally small furball. I've missed you, haven't I? Yes, I have."

Jhi gave the tentacle a friendly pat with one of her paws, then submitted graciously as the tentacle wound around her and gave an affectionate squeeze.

"It has been both quieter and more noisy in here without you," said Mulop. Another long tentacle lifted out of the water and indicated his great head. "You know what I mean."

Jhi inclined her own head sympathetically.

Essix descended into the cave with a flurry of wing flapping, landing on a boulder beside Rollan at the same time that Abeke held out her hand and released Uraza.

"All of you back," Mulop said, his tentacle moving over toward Uraza. The leopard growled at it. Unfazed, Mulop lifted his tentacle and waved it in a mirror image of Uraza's lashing tail. "Such a strange and lovely and terrible time. Aren't I thrilled beyond measure to see my four fallen siblings again? I am. And yet there is one I'd rather not see, but she is free, free as a snake, and so we come around again and all the old danger is new once more."

He drew his tentacles back into the water and subsided thoughtfully.

"Wait," Rollan said. "What?"

"Free as a snake?" Conor echoed alertly. "Are you talking about Gerathon?"

"Don't you know? Or is that a thing only I know? Ah, that is a thing I know. Maybe that is why I called you. My head is full of warnings, but which, but which is for you, that is the question."

"Um, I say give us all of them," Rollan volunteered. "All the warnings, please."

"Has Gerathon escaped from her prison?" Conor pressed.

"Most absolutely," Mulop said. Conor felt a horrible prickling all through his body, like dread was trying to flip his skin inside out.

"I thought that was impossible!" Abeke cried. "How did she get out?"

"My siblings specialize in the impossible," Mulop observed. "And no, clearly not impossible. Haven't you noticed her touch everywhere? She is the one who controls the drinkers of her Bile."

Beside Conor, Rollan gave a little start. Conor guessed that Rollan hadn't really thought about *who* was inside his mother, forcing her to try to kill Rollan.

"Do I think that is creepy?" Mulop went on. "I do, in fact. And I am an octopus. Creeping is a specialty of mine. But controlling the minds of others? I vastly disapprove. Ah, Feliandor," he added with a sigh, in what appeared to be a non sequitur, and suddenly fell silent again.

Conor exchanged a glance with Abeke. "Feliandor?" he prompted curiously. "Wasn't that—"

"The true name of the last Devourer," Meilin said, sounding horrified. She moved forward, the blue light reflecting off her smooth black hair. "Mulop, are you saying—was Feliandor controlled by the Bile? We were always taught that he started the war . . . but was Gerathon manipulating him the whole time?"

"Gerathon and Kovo," Mulop answered. "It was Kovo's idea. Oh, Kovo, I know about him. Clever brother, too clever, like me, but much more sinister. Take the young, ambitious king of Stetriol, offer him the world. Did I see that coming? I must admit I did not. A failure of vision, perhaps, but neither did you, right?" Mulop wagged a tentacle at Briggan like a scolding finger. "After all, who would have thought—who would *ever* have thought of giving that power to humans?" The octopus shuddered, sending ripples across the water.

"Feliandor was . . ." Rollan said. "That's it! That's what I saw in my dream on Nightshade Island! It was Kovo giving Feliandor the Bile—and then a real spirit animal came, and that's what destroyed the place and left all those, uh—"

"Echoes," Meilin finished for him. She reached out unconsciously and rested her hand on Jhi's back.

"I thought the war was the Devourer's idea, and Kovo and Gerathon were just helping him," Conor said.

"Far from it," Mulop said. "Kovo wanted to rule Erdas. Why? An excellent question. What do you do with an entire world once you have it? What is the point? Once you are done conquering, will you be happy? Because my guess is no, and so is mine. Ruling, controlling, dominating, power, all these mysterious needs. Perhaps it's a mammal thing. We Great Beasts do more than guard our talismans, you know. Do you know? I know, but then, who knows what others know. We also guard the secret of the bond between humans and spirit animals. That is the source of power. That is what Kovo tried to use, and will try to use again, to become king of all Erdas."

"But he can't!" Abeke protested. "He's locked up, and Halawir is guarding him. Isn't his prison even stronger than Gerathon's? If the Conquerors could release him, wouldn't they have done it already?"

Mulop stirred the water with his tentacles, blinking slowly at her. "Oh, they will. Kovo will be free before long, as well. Am I delighted about that? No, I am not. It is a strong prison, yes. Don't we all know how dangerous Kovo is? Weren't we there when he killed you four? No one even knew a Great Beast could be killed, but there you were, my brave fallen friends, and he did that. He is more powerful and dangerous than any of us, so we made his prison strong, but nothing can withstand everything. What does it take to destroy Kovo's prison?" He flipped a tentacle at the Granite Ram around Abeke's neck. "Talismans. The combined power of many talismans."

The octopus's gaze shifted to Conor, who thought guiltily of the Iron Boar. Was that the new Devourer's plan? Was that why the Conquerors were stealing talismans – to set Kovo free? What if the Iron Boar was the talisman that made the difference and brought down Kovo's prison walls?

"How many talismans do they have?" Conor asked.

"You are collecting talismans too," said Mulop. "That is a thing I know and you know. But how many more await you? Very few still remain with their Great Beasts. Tellun's. Cabaro's. And mine."

Conor and Abeke both gasped. "That's it?" Conor cried. "The Conquerors have all the others?"

"I did not say that," said Mulop cryptically. "But they control many, many things. You should perhaps hurry up and save the world. Here." He dipped his tentacles down into the blue water and lifted out a dripping wet black cord. At the end of it dangled an octopus carved from pale orange-pink coral.

"The Coral Octopus," Meilin said softly. She stumbled back and Rollan reached out to steady her. She brushed his hand away and rubbed her forehead with a confused, almost blank expression, her gaze fixed on the talisman.

"Isn't this what you came for?" asked Mulop. "I know it is. I give it to you freely. You need it, to fight Kovo and the others. He must be stopped; that is a thing we all know." His eyes somehow became stern. "Only you must not be careless and lose this one. I will know, and I will be very displeased, and so will I and also me."

"We'll be extremely careful," Conor promised.

Mulop extended the dangling talisman toward them.

Who should take it? Conor wondered. He glanced at his friends. Who could be trusted? He wanted to say *all of them*, but he was afraid that wasn't true. He wanted to let Abeke take it, just to show her he did trust her, but what if Meilin protested in front of Mulop and Mulop changed his mind about giving it to them?

Will they trust me *with it, after what happened with the Iron Boar?*

Rollan met his eyes and nodded, almost as if he knew what Conor was thinking. Abeke was watching the talisman, and Meilin shrugged, so Conor leaned forward and accepted it from Mulop's outstretched tentacle.

"Thank you," he said sincerely. "We really do need this."

"I know and know and know," the octopus said. "It's a very useful talisman. With this, you can breathe underwater and become gelatinous, like me, to fit through small spaces. Am I proud of it? Oh, rather. But I have one request before you leave with it. Is that so? It is. What do I want? A demonstration of your bravery. I will worry less if I can see what you are made of, friends of the Fallen."

Mulop shifted aside and indicated a part of the wall where the underwater light was brightest. "Down here is a hole that leads out to the ocean. It is about *so* big." He held up three tentacles to indicate a triangular space the size of a small watermelon. "I ask that one of you use my talisman to swim through there, out to the sea. Show me that you are willing, and my worry will be a small bit smaller."

"I'll do it," Conor said. Back into the water — he couldn't exactly claim to be excited about that. But it wasn't much for Mulop to ask in exchange for his talisman.

"Are you sure?" Abeke asked. "You'll be all right swimming that far?"

He nodded. "I'm not a great swimmer, but I *can* swim." He'd taught himself, more or less, like everyone did, in the ponds and rivers around Trunswick, where sometimes a sheep had to be rescued after a heavy rain. But splashing in a shallow stream with his brothers was not exactly the same as plunging into an entire vast ocean.

Don't think about sharks. Do NOT think about sharks.

Conor slipped the Coral Octopus around his neck, taking a deep breath.

"Friend of Briggan," Mulop said with a nod. He extended a tentacle for Briggan to sniff again. "Farewell, Pathfinder. I hope your destiny is brighter this time around."

Briggan let out a howl that echoed eerily around the walls of the cavern. As the echoes faded, he turned and nudged Conor's hand, then disappeared into his passive state.

"We'll go get the Kingray and bring him around to pick you up," Meilin said to Conor. She extended her hand briskly to Jhi.

Mulop stopped the panda with a gentle tentacle on one of her paws. "Old friend," he said. "There is another thing I know. And I am sorry."

Jhi shook her head, her silver eyes sad.

"What is it?" Meilin asked. "What do you mean?"

"It is a terrible thing," Mulop said. His deep green eyes bored into Meilin's. "You will wish you had been kinder, little warrior."

Meilin frowned, as though she wanted to argue but knew she shouldn't.

Mulop sank down into the water up to his eyes. "You'd better go, and quickly," he said. "Time is short, ships are long, and enemies are many, and it is a great burden you bear, tiny humans."

"Thank you again," Abeke said. Uraza flashed into passive state as well, and she turned to climb up the rocks.

"Good luck, Conor," Rollan said with a wave.

Conor sat on the edge of the rock and swung his legs into the glowing blue water. It felt warm with swirling currents of cold, and he could see far down into the depths of the grotto, where Mulop's tentacles coiled. There didn't seem to be a bottom; he felt like he might fall in and down and keep drifting for centuries.

He touched the Coral Octopus around his neck, took a deep breath, and plunged in.

The water closed over his head, cool and bubbling. His body immediately wanted to panic, to thrash and flail toward the air.

Trust the talisman. It was Mulop's voice and Tarik's voice and his own voice, all in his head, guiding him.

He forced himself to breathe in, even though his lungs were screaming, *No, it's water, you're going to die!*

One breath. Two breaths. No different from breathing

air, after all, although a part of him still rebelled at the sensation of water whooshing through his nose, his lungs, his mouth. Three breaths, four breaths, and it got a bit easier. His mind adjusted to the strangeness, and suddenly it was normal.

Well, perhaps not *normal,* exactly – he was underwater, but for once he didn't have to fear it. He couldn't drown, not with the Coral Octopus on. He could swim this way through the whole ocean, if he wanted to (as long as he avoided any *don't think about sharks*), and he'd never have to worry about the water closing over his head and dragging him down.

I wonder if I could even sleep underwater, he thought, a little giddily. His grandfather used to tell tales of water spirits that lived in lakes or rivers. *Now I could practically be one of them!*

Mulop's enormous bulk floated beside him, and Conor could see one tentacle pointing toward the exit, where a small beam of blue sunlight shone through. He paddled and kicked as hard as he could, wishing he were a better swimmer. He felt awkward and floppy next to Mulop's natural underwater grace.

Finally he reached the hole and grabbed the edges with his hands. The wall was rough, scraping his fingers, and the space was even smaller than he'd expected. It was an appalling prospect, wedging himself into such a tiny hole. His shoulders would never normally fit through there – but hopefully with the Coral Octopus they would.

What if the talisman didn't work as promised, though? What if he got halfway through and got *stuck* there, like a sheep trapped and waiting to be sheared?

He had to take a deep breath. The salty seawater burned the inside of his nose and his chest felt soggily heavy. If only the talisman gave one the grace of an octopus as well as its . . . squishiness.

As long as it does give me squishiness, I won't complain, Conor thought.

He had to stop worrying and just go.

Another breath, and then he drove his arms through first as though he were diving into the sunlit ocean outside. His head and shoulders stuck for a heart-stopping moment in the gap, and then his bones seemed to melt and squash together, and all at once he was squeezing through the hole like a sack of beans . . . or like an octopus.

Conor shoved himself free from the hole and felt his body go solid again. He was drifting in a wide blue emptiness with dazzling sunlight far above him. A small silver fish flashed by, then flashed back to peer at him curiously, then flashed away again. A few yards away, a giant turtle lazily swam past without giving him a second look.

I did it! We have Mulop's talisman!

Conor kicked vigorously, powering himself up to the surface as triumph flooded through him. For once, a Great Beast had been on their side; for once, things had gone as well as they possibly could. Maybe this was a sign that their luck was changing. Maybe they were close to stopping the Devourer. Maybe it could still happen before Kovo escaped his prison.

Conor's head broke the surface of the water and he sucked in a breath of real air. A cliff soared away over his head, with seagulls and hawks circling far up in the sky. Waves tugged him toward the rocks at the base of the cliff, and he had to kick and paddle just to stay where he was.

He twisted around, looking for the Kingray.

That's when he saw the ships.

There had to be at least a hundred of them, filling the sea to the horizons. As far as Conor could see, the entire island was surrounded. No giant stingray would be getting past this blockade, not with four kids on top of it.

They were trapped. Somehow the Conquerors had found them again.

I have to get back and warn the others.

But before Conor could move — before he could swim back to the cavern or even yell a warning — he suddenly felt something rubbery and slippery slither around his ankle. He had barely a moment to look down and see the long orange tentacles of Mulop, reaching up to drag him under.

And then the octopus yanked him down, down, down into the dark, bubbling depths of the sea.

15

BATTLE

ABEKE LOOKED DOWN FROM A LEDGE HIGH UP THE CAVERN wall and saw that Mulop and Conor had both vanished from the grotto. Dark ink was spreading through the clear blue water, hiding anything below it. She hoped Conor would be all right. She wondered if she should have volunteered instead.

The Granite Ram thumped against her chest as she leaped to the next rock, then the next. It was almost like flying, to feel so sure on her feet and be able to jump so far. In the space of a few breaths, she'd reached the top. She hauled herself onto the flat stone and collapsed there for a moment, feeling the sun on her face.

"Grrawk!"

Abeke opened her eyes and saw Essix beside her. The gyrfalcon peered meaningfully down into her face and blinked.

"Oh, sorry," she said, sitting up. She pulled the Granite

Ram over her head and handed it to Essix, who flew down into the hole to take it to Rollan.

Abeke stood up and stretched – and then froze.

"Rollan!" she shouted. "Meilin! Get up here, hurry!"

"Working on it," Rollan called.

"What's wrong?" came Meilin's voice.

"We're surrounded by Conquerors!" Abeke called back, her voice shaking. She pivoted, scanning the ocean. It was true; there were ships all around the island, each one swarming with people and animals.

How? her mind screamed. *How? How? How did they find us AGAIN?*

Pebbles cascaded below her, and Rollan's hand appeared. Abeke reached down and helped to drag him up beside her.

"See?" she said, pointing.

Rollan bent over, gasping for breath, and handed the Granite Ram to Essix again. A few moments later, Meilin scrambled up next to them. Ignoring Abeke's outstretched hand, she stood up and immediately began studying the ships, shading her eyes with one hand.

"How did they find us?" Rollan asked. "How do they *always* find us?"

"We already know the answer to that," Meilin pointed out. Her face was grim, and she didn't look at Abeke.

"All right, I know my mother said there was a mole," Rollan said. "But this was so fast! How could any of us have sent a message when we've all been together this whole time? On a stingray and then in Mulop's grotto? And none of us knew where we were going!"

"It's not even *possible*," Abeke said numbly. "There must be some other explanation, like something followed us, maybe—"

"Essix would have warned me if we were being followed," Rollan protested. "This makes no sense."

"There's nothing we can do about it now," Meilin retorted. "We have to get out of here."

"And we have to get Conor," Abeke interjected. *He must be terrified, floating out there in the sea with Conquerors' ships all around him.*

"Of course," Meilin said. She started down the rocky path to the beach. Abeke and Rollan followed as fast as they could, slipping and sliding on the loose rocks. There were scrubby bushes here and there, clinging to the patches of dirt, and Abeke found herself catching on to them whenever her feet slipped out from under her. The sunlight suddenly seemed unbearably hot, like the glare of ten thousand Conquerors' eyes watching them.

Below her, Meilin abruptly stopped, several yards above the beach. "Uh-oh," she murmured.

Three boats were just landing on the sand below them. As they watched, Conquerors began jumping out into the water and hauling the boats up onto the land. Their escape route was completely cut off.

Worse than that, they could see the entire blue bay from where they were—and there was no Kingray in sight.

"Did it just *leave* us?" Meilin hissed, staring down at the water.

"It was probably scared by all the ships arriving," Abeke said. "Or maybe it doesn't know anything about good and bad; maybe it figured now we'd have plenty of boats to carry us off the island."

"This is true," Meilin said. "Plenty of boats to carry us straight to Stetriol and into the hands of the Devourer. Aren't we lucky."

Abeke spotted a head of blond hair among the Conquerors moving below. A gasp escaped her before she could stop herself. *Shane! Shane is here!* Next to him she saw Zerif, right before Zerif looked up and spotted her.

For a chilling moment their eyes met, and then he yelled something to the Conquerors around him. They all turned to look up at the three kids on the cliff slope.

"That's not good," said Rollan.

With a shout of triumph, several Conquerors came racing up the beach toward them.

"Up, up, up!" Meilin cried. She drew her quarterstaff and released Jhi at the same time. "We'll have an advantage from the top of the cliff. Abeke, take the Granite Ram!"

Startled, Abeke reached out and caught the talisman as Meilin tossed it to her.

"Get as high as you can and use your bow," Meilin ordered. "Go! Now!"

Abeke didn't argue. She slipped the ram over her neck and released Uraza, then leaped rapidly from boulder to boulder up the slope. As she jumped, she pulled out her bow, and when she reached a flat spot, she whirled and fired down into the mass of Conquerors below.

She could see at once that the enemy had planned ahead for this attack, at least in choosing which spirit animals would come over in the boats to the island. Most of the animals swarming rapidly up the rocks were monkeys and apes, perfectly suited to climbing. Long-armed gibbons clambered after macaques with enormous teeth. A pair of baboons shrieked furiously, and three monkeys Abeke had no name for were advancing relentlessly up the steepest part of the cliff, their faces strange and dark. They were all unnaturally big and angry.

Abeke aimed at one with matted fur and blazing eyes as it scurried toward Rollan. Her arrow sent it flying backward off the cliff with an unearthly scream. Another arrow thudded through one of the baboons; her third narrowly missed a snarling chimpanzee.

Not far below her, Uraza was grappling with a huge doglike creature that Abeke thought might be a dingo. The leopard had her jaws locked around its neck while it thrashed and clawed at her.

Jhi had retreated up the rocks, but Meilin was clearly using her heightened senses as she fought. She looked like a blur of motion, swinging her quarterstaff to knock aside enemies and in the next moment launching a flurry of kicks to drive them back. It was supernatural how fast she was moving.

Scanning the attackers, Abeke spotted a black shape scrambling up the rocks toward Jhi. It looked like a bear, but with a bright yellow arc of fur on its chest. A sun bear, if she remembered correctly from the books of animals Tarik had shown her on the ship. It growled at Jhi, flexing long, cruel-looking claws.

There was no time for Meilin to get to Jhi to protect her. Abeke whipped her bow around and launched an arrow straight into the sun bear's distinctive markings. It roared furiously and toppled off the rocks.

She felt a small glow of satisfaction, but it flared out quickly. There were so many Conquerors—so many Bile-enslaved animals. How could Abeke, Rollan, and Meilin possibly fight them all off and escape, especially without the Kingray? And what about Conor, floundering out in the ocean, waiting for them to come get him? Would he be all right, or would the Conquerors grab him too? What if they had more of their deadly sharks in the water?

Maybe we should surrender, she thought hopelessly. *If I could talk to Shane—maybe he'd even let us go. At least he'd save Conor. And he'd make sure our spirit animals stay safe.* She thought so, at least. She couldn't see where he'd disappeared to in the chaos of people below.

But that would put three more talismans in the Devourer's hands. Would that be enough to free Kovo? Would that mean the end of Erdas as they knew it?

A yowl of beastly fury dragged Abeke's attention back to the battle. She fired three more arrows in quick succession at a tiger, a hyena, and another giant monkey, missing one but hitting the other two. She felt for another arrow and realized she'd be out soon.

I need to make these really count.

She narrowed her eyes, searching the horde of people below.

There he is.

Zerif.

He'd lied to her; he'd tried to turn her evil. Zerif was the leader, or at least *a* leader of the Conquerors. Maybe if she could take him down, they'd fall back and give up – or at least be confused enough that Abeke and her friends might have a chance of escaping.

She drew her bow back and aimed, trying to ignore her thudding heart. The man stood on an outcropping, shouting orders at the fighters scrambling up behind him. Her sharp arrow tip was pointed directly down at Zerif's heart.

It was one thing to shoot gibbons and tigers – but deliberately aiming at someone she knew, someone she had spoken to . . . Wouldn't that make her as evil as any of them? She shivered, and then tightened her arm muscles, trying to turn herself to stone. *I have to. It's the only way to stop them. Even if it's wrong.*

And then Meilin will know I'm truly a Greencloak.

She took another deep breath, stilling the tremors running along her arms. And then, strong as a lion, fierce as a leopard, brave as a warrior, cold as a glacier – she fired the hardest shot she'd ever taken. The arrow took a little bit of her with it.

It struck Zerif right in the chest, exactly where his malevolent heart beat.

And bounced off.

Abeke gasped. *That's impossible!* She knew her aim had been straight and true. It should have killed him instantly.

Zerif turned slowly, rubbing his chest as if he'd been pinged with a button. He glanced down at the arrow. A gloating smile spread across his face, and he raised his eyes to meet Abeke's.

She watched numbly as he reached into the collar of

his shirt and held up something that gleamed dully in the sunshine.

The Iron Boar.

That's what it does, she realized with anguish. *The Iron Boar — it must make your skin as tough and leathery as a boar's hide, like a kind of invisible armor. My arrows will never pierce it. Zerif is indestructible right now.*

Zerif tucked the Iron Boar back into his shirt, still grinning smugly. Abeke wanted to smash something. Ideally his face.

Instead she whipped more arrows out and shot the closest three creatures, one after the other in a furious whirl. The front line of attackers fell back for a moment, and Rollan seized the chance to climb higher, toward Abeke.

"I know how we can get off this island!" he shouted to her.

"Look out!" Meilin cried.

Rollan staggered sideways as if he'd been punched by the air, and then crashed forward into the rock wall. Abeke spotted nearly invisible ripples in the air around him and realized someone was using the Crystal Polar Bear.

She scanned the mass of attackers until she spotted the woman with the talisman. It was the massive woman from Sunlight Island, the one who'd been bonded to the Komodo dragon. She had a look of pure hatred on her face, and she stood on a ledge not far from Rollan with the Crystal Polar Bear glittering around her neck. Her arm swept out and Rollan was nearly knocked down the cliff, but at the last moment his hand shot out and caught on to one of the ragged bushes.

Before the woman could strike again, Meilin's knife skewered her hand and she screamed with pain and anger. A heartbeat later, Essix dropped from the sky and drove her talons and beak at the Conqueror's face. The woman fled back down the cliff, arms over her head.

"Quick, Rollan!" Abeke called. She leaped down to him, light as the wind, and dragged him up onto solid ground. Meilin was not far behind, and they all scrambled up the rock face together.

"I know what to do," Rollan said again, wiping sweat from his forehead. "At least, I hope it's an option. Abeke, do you have the Slate Elephant?"

She couldn't believe she'd forgotten something so important. Kalani had handed it back to her before swimming away with Katoa. Abeke dug into her pocket, trying not to meet the hard stare coming from Meilin's eyes, and handed the elephant to Rollan.

"Thank all the Great Beasts," Rollan said with immense relief. "Except for the bad two, I mean. Essix!"

"We can fly away!" Abeke cried. "That's brilliant!"

"Why didn't you think of it sooner?" Meilin demanded. She held out her arm. "Jhi, come quickly." The panda scrambled over, paused for a moment with an odd, heartbroken look in her silver eyes, and then vanished into the tattoo on Meilin's hand.

Abeke glanced anxiously down the slope and saw Uraza pin a giant owl under her claws. The leopard looked up, sensing Abeke's attention. She swatted the owl away and came bounding up the rocks toward them.

"We're going to fly," Abeke told her, holding out her

arm. "My guess is you'd like this even less than being on a boat."

Uraza growled in agreement, lashing her tail. She turned her violet gaze on the Conquerors climbing toward them and apparently decided they had enough time to escape. A moment later, she had also disappeared into passive state.

By then Essix was swooping down. Rollan climbed up toward her, clutching the elephant talisman.

"We can do this," Abeke said to Meilin, nearly falling over with relief. "Essix can take us down to pick up Conor and then we can really get away, with the talismans and everything."

Meilin had her head turned away, toward the Conquerors. She didn't answer for a moment, but when she turned back to Abeke, there was a strange blank expression on her face.

And her eyes were yellow.

"I'm afraid you and I are not going anywhere," she said to Abeke. "We have an appointment with the Reptile King."

16

BETRAYAL

ONE MOMENT, MEILIN WAS FIGHTING.

Time had slowed down and she was flowing between moments, striking out with her staff one way, blocking an attack from the other direction, kicking a chimpanzee back into his Conqueror. She was in control of everything. She felt like she could almost steer the wind to do what she wanted. She could take down every enemy on the island single-handedly, if she chose to.

And then, as she climbed up toward Abeke and Rollan, she felt her eyesight blur for a moment. She hesitated, blinking—and her hand began to move by itself.

Shocked, Meilin tried to freeze in place.

But her feet betrayed her, taking another step, and another, closer and closer to her friends.

What is happening? Meilin could only watch in horror. She wanted to scream, but even her voice wasn't hers anymore. It felt like her blood had turned into something alien, slithering around chillingly inside her. She was trapped in her own body, helpless, as it scrambled up the last few boulders and stood beside Abeke.

As if from a long way away, she heard Abeke say, "We can really get away, with the talismans and everything."

Not so fassssst, said another voice in Meilin's head – not her own. *Someone else is in my head!* She needed to shout a warning to the others, but something else was coming out of her mouth. Cold, dangerous words. Words of betrayal and darkness. "An appointment with the Reptile King." *What does that mean?*

How is this happening?

Rollan! Rollan, pay attention! Stop me!

But Rollan was focused on Essix, who couldn't land where they were if she was going to get bigger. He was ascending away from them, to a higher, clear spot where they could climb aboard the falcon and escape.

Except nobody is escaping today.

Her hand – her disloyal, traitorous hand – shot out and grabbed Abeke's arm, fingers pressing into Uraza's mark.

"Come with me," she heard her voice growl. "If you release Uraza, she will be dead before you can take another breath."

"Meilin!" Abeke cried. "What are you doing?" She tried to struggle, but Meilin's grip was too strong. "Rollan!" she screamed.

Rollan finally, finally turned to look at them.

His face – Meilin knew she would have nightmares about his face forever. She could see as clear as day the moment when he realized that Meilin was betraying them.

But it's not me, she tried to shout. *I would never do this!*

And yet at the same time she was dragging Abeke down the slope toward the Conquerors. Abeke was taller, but Meilin knew ways of holding people that made it almost impossible for her to break free.

"Meilin!" Rollan shouted. "Stop! What are you—"

He must have figured it out at the same time that she did.

Bile. Someone gave me Bile instead of Nectar at my ceremony. And now Gerathon can control me.

Worse: She'd been able to control Meilin this whole time. She'd seen through her eyes, knew everything she knew.

It's me. I'm *the mole.*

Her insides felt like they were splintering apart, crashing down like the walls of Jano Rion.

She had a sudden, ghastly memory of her father's death and his last words to her as his blood stained the grass of the battlefield near Dinesh's temple.

Should have told you . . . betrayed . . . the Bile.

Did he know?

She remembered how convinced, how *certain* he had been that she would call a spirit animal on the day of her Nectar Ceremony.

That led to a thought she couldn't bear, so awful it was like having her heart ripped out by the Devourer's crocodile.

Did my father *do this to me?*

Rollan raced down the rocks toward them, sliding and scattering pebbles in his haste.

"Stay back!" Meilin-but-not-Meilin yelled. She flipped Abeke around in front of her and pressed a knife to her throat.

No, no, no, the real Meilin sobbed inside herself.

Rollan froze, several paces away but close enough to see her eyes.

"Meilin," he called. Pain was carved all over his face. Meilin knew he must be thinking of his mother, and how he'd been facing her and the same evil yellow eyes only a short time ago. "Listen to me. I know you're still in there. You can fight this! You're the strongest person I – the strongest person maybe *ever*. You can fight her!"

Meilin didn't think that was true. What chance did she have against a Great Beast and her magic? But she tried. She dug mental claws into the sides of her brain and shoved, trying to force her way out and back into control of her own body.

Her feet wavered underneath her, and her grip on Abeke loosened. The Niloan girl suddenly twisted under Meilin's arm and jerked free. She bolted three steps up the slope toward Rollan.

And then Meilin's quarterstaff came down on her head with a heart-stopping crack.

Abeke collapsed to the ground like a doll.

Meilin stared at her body, horrified. *I hope she's only unconscious.*

"Abeke!" Meilin's real voice struggled out and was crushed in almost the same breath. "There is no one who can fight me," she snarled at Rollan. She advanced to stand over Abeke's fallen body. "Certainly not your precious Meilin, who's been my puppet from the moment she summoned Jhi."

The sleepwalking, Meilin realized. *Every time I blacked out, that was Gerathon taking control of my body.*

Which meant she could take control without Meilin even knowing it. And that also meant she *did* want Meilin to know it now. She wanted Meilin to suffer through the betrayal of her friends and be aware of every moment of it.

Meilin felt her mouth being forced into a cruel smile. Her voice had an unnatural hiss to it as Gerathon spoke to Rollan again. "Didn't you ever wonder about how easily she controls that panda? Their bond is a Bile bond. Jhi has no choice but to obey her."

Inside herself, Meilin wanted to curl up and die. The way she ordered Jhi around – the way Jhi always tried so hard to do as she was asked – now it was painfully clear, horribly wrong. She'd thought she was so great, such a natural leader that of course Jhi would follow her. She'd mocked the others for having trouble with their spirit animals. She'd assumed that was just another way she was superior, as with her fighting skills.

But it was all a lie. Their connection was forced, not a true bond. Jhi was being controlled by Meilin exactly the way Meilin was being controlled by Gerathon right now.

She felt like throwing up, but she couldn't even move.

My poor Jhi. I'm so sorry. Is this what it always felt like, being with me? Did you feel trapped and enslaved? Do you hate me?

She remembered Mulop's words to Jhi. *He must have known. Seems like that would have been one of the more useful warnings to pass along, octopus.*

Her body was bending and lifting Abeke against her will. She dragged the taller girl up to a sitting position, and out of the corner of her eye she saw the flash of something gray around her neck.

The talisman! Meilin thought. *NO. They can't have me and Abeke* and *the Granite Ram too.*

With all the will she had left in the world, she shoved outward as if she were forcing herself through an invisible hedge. Stabbing, scratching pain seared through her, but she seized control of one hand — that's all she needed, just one arm — ripped the cord off Abeke's neck, and threw it as hard as she could at Rollan.

"Get out of here!" she screamed while she still could.

Shocked, he fumbled to catch the talisman and then took a step back. But his haunted eyes were still on her face. "No, Meilin. We can get you away from here. We can *help you!*"

"You know you can't," she answered, the one thing both she and Gerathon agreed on. It wasn't safe for her to be anywhere near Rollan or the talismans or the Greencloaks. The Great Serpent could control her at any moment, could spy on them whenever she wanted to. Meilin had to give herself to the Conquerors to protect her friends.

She let go of the last bit of resistance and stepped back.

But apparently now Gerathon had decided she wanted them all. Meilin found her body dropping Abeke and then running up the rocks toward Rollan, knives out and ready to attack.

"I'm not abandoning you!" Rollan shouted, his face going hard.

He tackled her to the ground, knocking the knives away, and they wrestled in the dirt, kicking and twisting. But Meilin was better trained, faster, more wily. In moments, she was able to flip him over and pin him to the ground. She felt herself drawing another knife from her boot.

Rollan, Rollan, please run. Please get away from here. Take your talismans and fly.

He knew what a skilled fighter she was. He didn't stand a chance against her.

Meilin flung herself against the walls of the prison around her mind, screaming and kicking. For a moment her hands paused, and in that moment Rollan was able to throw her off and squirm free.

And then he did run, and he didn't look back.

Gerathon wanted to chase him, Meilin could feel it. But Rollan threw the Granite Ram around his neck and leaped away with all the speed and grace of Arax the Ram. On the cliff top, Essix was waiting; it would only take a moment for Rollan to switch talismans, climb on board, and escape.

Gerathon hissed through Meilin's teeth, then turned and kicked Abeke in the side. "At least we have these two," she growled. With unnatural strength, Meilin crouched and threw Abeke over her shoulder.

The Conquerors were waiting for them. Someone took Abeke from Meilin as she stepped down the rocky path. Her feet propelled her onto the once-beautiful white sand of the beach, now trampled by a thousand paws and marred with blotches of blood.

Zerif stood by one of the boats with his jackal beside him, smirking. He gave Meilin a small, ironic bow as she walked up to him.

"Nice of you to join us at last," he said. "Of course, you've been terribly useful on the other side. We all appreciate that. But now that we have so many talismans, it's time for you to stand by the Reptile King, where you belong."

Something in her face made him pause. He tugged on his beard, frowning.

"You did bring a talisman, didn't you? The Coral Octopus, I hope? Or the Granite Ram would do. I can see you don't have the Slate Elephant."

Meilin turned and followed his gaze to the sky, where the enormous shape of Essix was winging away to the north. Rollan was just a small dark blur, crouched on the falcon's back.

"No talismans," Gerathon said harshly in Meilin's voice. "But we have Jhi and Uraza, and Tellun remains hidden. The only talisman left for them to find is Cabaro's. Our plan is nearly complete. Kovo will be free soon, and then your Reptile King's armies will lay waste to the last rebellious corners of Erdas."

Meilin spotted Shane hovering over the next boat as Abeke was lifted inside. Shackles were snapped over Abeke's wrists and ankles.

"Careful, be gentle," Shane protested, sounding guilty.

Meilin automatically began to raise her arms, ready for her own shackles.

In her head, Gerathon started laughing. *You don't need*

shackles, drinker of the Bile, the serpent's voice hissed. *You're my creature. Try to resist all you like, but in the end, I control you completely.*

Despair washed over her. She stepped into the boat beside Zerif and watched Mulop's island grow smaller and smaller as they rowed toward the Conquerors' ships. Gerathon could keep her eyes open, could point them in any direction she chose, but she couldn't stop the tears that slowly rolled down Meilin's face.

I'm the mole. Not Abeke. Not anyone else. Me.

I'm the reason the Conquerors are winning the war. I'm the reason they've always been able to find us; it's my fault they have the talismans they stole from us.

It's my fault my father is dead.

And now that I know Gerathon can control me . . . it's as though there's no Meilin left at all.

17

GONE

ROLLAN CIRCLED OVER THE OCEAN AND THE FLEET OF SHIPS for as long as he dared, but he saw no sign of Conor in the water, even with his falcon-enhanced sight.

Please let him be all right. Don't let him be lost too.

He couldn't have drowned with the Coral Octopus on . . . could he? Had one of the Conquerors' ships picked him up? Or something worse . . . Rollan could see the menacing fins of Bile-enhanced sharks lurking between the ships. He wouldn't let his imagination go any further in that direction.

Rollan didn't want to leave him. He didn't want to leave Meilin or Abeke either, but how could he get anywhere near Zerif's ship?

What can I do? Of all of us to get away . . . I'm the most useless.

Finally one of the Conquerors' arrows came too close, and he was forced to tell Essix to fly away. He didn't want to risk losing her too, and he could feel the weight of the talismans he carried, one around his neck and one in his pocket. The only thing left that he could do was take those talismans to safety.

Sick at heart, he leaned into Essix's warm feathers, feeling her muscles contract and lengthen below him as she flew. The cold wind whipped away the tears on his cheeks.

It seemed like a long time later when he felt Essix tilt her wings to descend. He looked up and realized that the sun was setting. Golden light spilled across the rippling sea. The sky was streaked with blazes of pink and orange.

It was the most beautiful and the saddest sunset he'd ever seen.

Essix soared down toward the *Tellun's Pride*, now anchored off a small deserted island. Tarik must have ordered the ship to move so he wouldn't come into contact with Kalani's people — protecting them from *tapu* again. The huge shapes of the rockback whales loomed beside the ship, as big as islands themselves.

As the giant falcon spiraled down toward the deck, the sailors on board began shouting and pointing. Rollan spotted Tarik's familiar green cloak as the man climbed onto the deck. Tarik shaded his face to look up at Rollan and waved, and Rollan was startled to feel more tears pricking at the backs of his eyes. He leaned forward, too defeated to wave back.

There wasn't enough room for Essix to land on the ship without getting tangled in the masts, so she swooped close enough to hover while Rollan swung himself into the rigging. As soon as he was secure, he took off the Slate Elephant and climbed down to where Tarik was waiting.

The Greencloak's face was openly relieved, until he saw Rollan's expression.

"What happened?" he asked, panic creeping into his voice. He reached up unconsciously to stroke Lumeo's back, worry lines creasing his forehead. "Where are the others? Rollan?" He caught Rollan as the boy staggered away from the ropes. *"Where are the others?"*

"I lost them," Rollan said. His legs gave up on standing and he crumpled to the deck. He buried his face in his hands, leaning against his knees. "Tarik, Meilin was the mole. She took Abeke. The Conquerors have them both now." He looked up into Tarik's shocked eyes. "She – she's being controlled by Gerathon. Somebody gave her the Bile." A flood of anger washed over him. "Somebody gave her the *Bile*, Tarik!" he yelled. "How could that happen? It must have been at her Nectar Ceremony. Who could have done that? Why didn't the Greencloaks protect her?"

Tarik crouched beside him and put one hand on Rollan's shoulder. "Rollan, if Meilin was being controlled by Gerathon, I'm sure there was nothing you could have done to save her or Abeke. This isn't your fault."

"I know that!" Rollan shouted, shaking him off. "It's the Greencloaks' fault for letting her drink the Bile in the first place!"

Tarik rubbed his face with his hands, looking far older than he was. "Where's Conor?"

"He had the Coral Octopus," Rollan mumbled, dropping his head again. "He swam into the sea and then – I don't know. I couldn't find him. There were too many Conquerors and he wasn't anywhere. . . ."

"We'll go back and find him," Tarik promised. "Lenori may be able to sense Briggan, or ask for a vision, or—"

"That won't be necessary," said a tired voice.

They both whirled around and saw Conor climbing over the rail, dripping wet.

"Conor!" Rollan cried. He wasn't sure he'd ever been so happy to see someone. He scrambled to his feet and nearly toppled the boy over as he hugged him. "How did you get away? How did you get *here*?"

"It was Mulop," Conor said, looking more than a little embarrassed. "He followed me out through the hole, grabbed me, and dragged me under the Conquerors' ships. It took me a while to realize he wasn't, like, taking me off to eat me or something. He just wanted to make sure the Coral Octopus was safe." Conor touched the talisman around his neck. "We traveled underwater most of the way here." He shivered. A puddle had already formed around his feet.

Tarik pulled off his own cloak to put around Conor's shoulders. He paused for a moment, gave Conor a fierce hug of his own, and then went to get dry clothes and towels.

"I'm glad you guys are safe too," Conor said to Rollan while they waited. "I was really worried about you, but Mulop wouldn't go back. He said, 'I won't risk the Coral Octopus falling into the wrong tentacles, and neither will I.' I think maybe he knew the ships were out there and set up the whole test so he could follow me out through the hole and get at least one of us to safety with his talisman. I'm sorry it was me, though; I wish I could have stayed to help you guys. Did you use the Slate Elephant on Essix? That's what I was think – Rollan? What is it? What's wrong?"

Rollan shook his head, took a deep breath, and told Conor everything about the battle and the truth about Meilin.

Conor stared at him in disbelief, his green eyes wide and confused. After a moment, he held out his arm and Briggan appeared. Conor crouched beside the wolf, wrapped his arm around Briggan's neck, and leaned into his fur. Briggan licked Conor's hand and made a soft whining sound.

"Poor Meilin," Conor whispered.

"It's not right," Rollan said furiously. "The Bile is – it's unnatural and wrong and . . . and awful. No one should be able to control people that way. And Meilin must have been *tricked* into drinking it, which makes it even worse. . . ."

"Even worse than your mom," Conor finished the thought.

Rollan was trying really hard not to think about his mom. He was trying not to remember those same serpentine yellow eyes looking out of Aidana's and Meilin's faces. That same malevolent presence forcing people he cared about to try to kill him. The same struggle he'd seen on both faces, as Aidana and Meilin both tried so desperately to break free and save him.

Tarik returned with blankets for both of them. Darkness was spreading over the ship, and stars were beginning to emerge one by one in the purple sky.

"What do we do now?" Conor asked Tarik. The three of them stood at the railing, watching the Hundred Isles slip past them. "Can we rescue Abeke? Is there anything we can do to . . . to fix Meilin?"

"I don't know," Tarik said heavily.

"There must be," Rollan said, digging his nails into the wood. "There *must* be a way to reverse the effects of the Bile."

"If there is, we'll find it," Conor agreed. With a stab of anguish, Rollan remembered Meilin saying almost those exact words.

Essix landed on the railing and sidled up beside Rollan. She eyed him thoughtfully for a moment, then hopped onto his shoulder and tugged on a lock of his hair.

"At least we have the Coral Octopus," Tarik murmured, but from the tone of his voice Rollan knew they felt the same way.

The talisman wasn't worth it. No talisman could be worth the price that Oceanus had exacted from them.

Meilin and Abeke were in the hands of the Devourer.

And according to Mulop, Kovo would soon be free.

Rollan stared bleakly down at the black ocean.

Was there any hope left for Erdas?

Tui T. Sutherland

is a *Jeopardy!* champion and the author of the dragon series Wings of Fire, the Menagerie trilogy, the Pet Trouble series, and three books in the bestselling Seekers series (as part of the Erin Hunter team). Right now she has just one dog (clearly her spirit animal, Sunshine), but growing up she had, at various times, piglets in the bathtub, shrieking monkeys in the backyard, and a kitten with super-villain plans. She lives in Massachusetts with her husband, two sons, and Sunshine.

Visit her online at www.tuibooks.com.

THE 39 CLUES

THE STUNNING ADVENTURE FROM BESTSELLING AUTHOR
RICK RIORDAN

Available in print and eBook editions

scholastic.com/the39clues

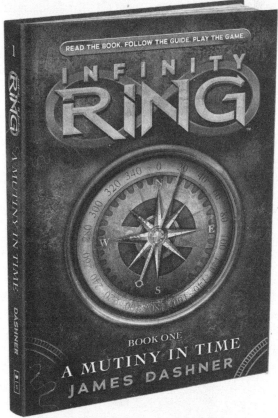

BOOK SIX:

RISE AND FALL

Deep in a vast desert waits one of the most
powerful and dangerous of all the Great Beasts:
Cabaro the Lion. With the team shattered,
stealing the giant lion's talisman seems
impossible. But what choice do they have?

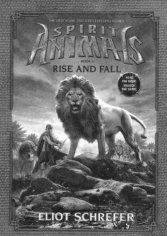

Each book unlocks in-game rewards.
Log in with your copy to help save Erdas!

The Legend Lives in You

scholastic.com/spiritanimals